RICHARD HAPPER

365
REASONS TO BE
PROUD TO BE A
LONDONER

PORTICO

To the 15 grotty flatmates, 7 demented bosses, 1 police raid and 1,354 lost lunchtimes that made living in London such an absolute blast.

First published in the United Kingdom in 2015 by
Portico
1 Gower Street
London
WC1E 6HD

An imprint of Pavilion Books Company Ltd
Copyright © Pavilion Books Company Ltd 2015

ISBN 978-1-91023-206-4

A CIP catalogue record for this book is available from the British Library.

10 9 8 7 6 5 4 3 2 1

Reproduction by ColourDepth
Printed and bound by Toppan Leefung Printing Ltd, China

This book can be ordered direct from the publisher at
www.pavilionbooks.com

'Sir, when a man is tired of London, he is tired of life; for there is in London all that life can afford.'
Samuel Johnson

*'You are now
In London, that great sea, whose ebb and flow
At once is deaf and loud, and on the shore
Vomits its wrecks, and still howls on for more.
Yet in its depth what treasures!'*
Percy Bysshe Shelley

'I don't know what London's coming to – the higher the buildings the lower the morals.'
Noël Coward

INTRODUCTION

London was the capital of the world's first industrialised country, the first modern mega-city of more than one million inhabitants, and the largest city in the world for 125 years.

This was the heart of the Empire on which the sun never set and although those days are long gone it is no surprise that you can hear more languages spoken here (over 300) than in any other city.

This cultural capital has been home to more creative, dynamic and inventive people than any other metropolis on Earth. From Wolfgang Amadeus Mozart to Jimi Hendrix, they came *here* to make it big. London's West End is the world's most concentrated entertainment centre, with 40 theatres showing exciting and entertaining dramas (and *The Mousetrap*). The National Gallery, Royal Society and British Museum are institutions that other countries would give their left Jackson Pollock to have.

As may be expected for the greenest city of its size on the planet, it's the spiritual home of several sports including cricket, hockey, tennis, table tennis, polo and roller-skating.

Over 20 chemical elements were discovered here, and the notion of the nuclear chain reaction dropped into a scientist's head as he watched the traffic on Southampton Row. The city's traffic, incidentally, was so horrendous even in 1863 that the world's first, and still one of the biggest, underground railways was built.

A mighty mother of invention, London has inspired world-changing creations including penicillin, television (first publicly demonstrated in Selfridges), the miniskirt, the circus, daily newspapers, canned food, the Christmas card and the jigsaw puzzle.

While it has a magnificent past, today London is looking to an even brighter future. It is home to the tallest building in the European Union and in 2012 showed the world how an Olympic Games should really be done. While Boris's Bikes will solve the transport problem once and for all.

To live, work, laugh and love in this place takes a special sort of person. Londoners withstood three solid months of daily bombing in the Blitz, and not only didn't give in, but came back stronger. London is an exciting, infuriating, invigorating, fun, dirty, historic, weird and unpredictable place to live and work.

And it's all yours.

JANUARY

CHEQUE OUT THIS NEW IDEA

1 We can be supremely proud that London is officially the world's most popular tourist destination – 16 million overseas visitors in 2014, and every single bloody one of them on the Central Line at 8.15am. So it's fitting that the city invented the traveller's cheque. They were first issued today in 1772 by the London Credit Exchange Company, and could be used in 90 European cities. The first one was lost in Paris two days later by a posh kid doing the Grand Tour on his gap year.

EVERYTHING THAT'S IN IT

On the wall of the players' entrance to Centre Court at Wimbledon is a very special poem – 'If' by Rudyard Kipling. It's the world's most quoted verse and probably its most rousing. Its quiet wisdom, a reflection on the beauty of living a virtuous and humble life, was actually inspired by a colonial raid executed by Sir Leander Starr Jameson in the Transvaal province of South Africa, which finished on this day in 1896. The raid was a bloody disaster and its failure helped incite the Second Boer War. Still, the poem is jolly nice.

THE ORIGINAL LADS' MAG

The world's first-ever magazine, *The Gentleman's Magazine*, was published in Clerkenwell today in 1731 by printer Edward Cave. His idea was for a periodical that covered all topics of gentlemanly general interest, from business to fiction. The use of 'magazine' came from the French for 'storehouse', and it ran for nearly 200 years. Dr Samuel Johnson got his first job as a writer on the periodical, and it had all the ingredients of the similar modern mag: articles, dramatic images, stories and special offers – all it lacked was a cover with a woodcut of a wench with her bosom bursting out.

BUT MONSIEUR, *LONDON* IS THE CENTRE OF THE WORLD

You think train timetables are tricky to read nowadays, but in the early 19th century most cities, and countries, had their own idea of what time it was. With faster trains and increased international trade this became a nightmare – a definitive world time was essential. The meridian at Greenwich observatory was established today in 1851 and later accepted as the planet's prime meridian. Longitude and time zones have been aligned with London ever since. Greenwich got the nod because 72 per cent of the world's commerce depended on British sea-charts – and because it annoyed the French intensely. They went into a cream puff and kept using the Paris meridian until 1914.

YOU YOU CAN CAN SAY SAY THAT THAT AGAIN AGAIN

Hampstead-born electrical engineer Alan Blumlein went to see a film with his wife today in 1931, and got annoyed. Not because of teenagers snogging, but because cinemas then only had a single set of speakers – Blumlein thought it odd that the actor's voice came from the left when his face was on the right-hand side of the screen. He had a point. Blumlein told his wife that he would fix that problem and promptly went back to his lab and invented stereo sound, which he patented later that year. The worlds of cinema and music would never sound the same again.

PLEASE ADJUST YOUR DRESS
BEFORE LEAVING

6 The Duke of Wellington's statue in front of the Royal Exchange stands as a dignified memorial to the great soldier. Slightly less dignified, although surely as historically notable, the statue is also the site of the world's first underground toilets, which were built in 1885, right beneath the plinth itself. They were completed today and opened soon after – but only for gentlemen. Ladies had to contain themselves, ask at railway stations or just not even think about something so vulgar.

COOL MOOVES

Ice-skating was strictly a winter sport before John Gamgee opened his Glaciarium in London today in 1876. This was the world's first artificial ice rink and it owed its success to cows. Well, their hair. To freeze the water, Gamgee ran a solution of glycerine, ether, nitrogen peroxide and water through copper pipes packed in insulating layers of earth, wood and cow hair. The water went over that and was quickly frozen, allowing people to skid about on top till the cows came home.

FLOATING IN A MOST-A PECULIAR WAY

Long before Lady Gaga was reinventing herself every other dinner-time, pop's original chameleon was blazing a culture-changing trail. Ziggy Stardust, the Thin White Duke, Aladdin Sane, David Robert Jones – or David Bowie as we know him best – was born today in 1947 and first hit the charts in 1969. After 45 years and 140 million albums, it's hard to remember just how weird and wonderful Bowie was – he really seemed like he was from another planet. And we can be proud he was from Brixton, which in many ways is not of this Earth.

OI, COCO, IF THE WOKING TRAIN'S CANCELLED I'M NOT LAUGHING

If it sometimes feels like Waterloo is run by a bunch of clowns that may be because the world's first modern circus was established here. In what was then a field, horseman Philip Astley first performed his acrobatic riding show on this day in 1768. Astley was the first to have his horses run in a circle, which put the action in the centre of the crowd and generated centrifugal force to give the rider stability. His ring diameter of 42ft (12.8m) is still standard today. He also introduced clowns to keep the punters chuckling between the acts.

THE TRAILBLAZING TUBE

Strap-hanging in 100-degree heat on the Piccadilly Line might not immediately fill you with pride, but it should. In the 1850s, over 200,000 workers flooded into London every day, sending traffic into a spasm. So the city leaders hatched a scheme to alleviate the gridlock forever: the Metropolitan Railway, the world's first underground railway line. It opened today in 1863 and didn't quite remove congestion, but it did prove rather popular. Today, London's Tube is still one of the biggest metros in the world, with 270 stations and more than a billion passenger journeys each year.

IT COULD BE YE

The very first national lottery was chartered by Queen Elizabeth I and drawn at the west door of St Paul's, today in 1569. It was to raise money for the 'reparation of the havens and strength of the Realme, and towardes such other publique good workes'. The government deficit, in other words. The government later went on to sell lottery ticket rights to brokers, who then hired agents and runners to sell them. These brokers eventually became modern-day stockbrokers.

IN OCTAVIA WE TRUST

Octavia Hill was a social reformer who joined with solicitor Robert Hunter and clergyman Hardwicke Rawnsley in London today in 1894 to form the National Trust. Since then the Trust has saved many of England's best-loved buildings and landscapes from ruin, or worse, being sold to the highest bidder. It owns 200 historic houses, 1.5 per cent of the total land in England, Wales and Northern Ireland) and has 3.7 million members. It has inspired dozens of similar organisations around the world. Hill also invented the term 'Green Belt' and stopped Hampstead Heath and Parliament Hill Fields from being built on.

MEDICAL MARVEL FROM THE MIDDLE AGES

Patients have been lying on stretchers in the corridors of St Barts longer than in any hospital in Europe. Since 1123, in fact. Henry VIII later ensured it got some much-needed cash and gave it to 'the citizens of London and their successors for ever' today in 1547. William Harvey first revealed the wonders of the circulatory system here in the 17th century, and major surgical advances were made in the 18th. Still on its original site, it has survived the Great Fire and the Blitz. But will it survive the Tory party, we ask ourselves?

MIME IS MONEY

It's by far the world's most famous festival of its type, but hardly anyone's heard of it – which might be because it's the London International Mime Festival. It had humble beginnings today in 1977, starting when a guy in white gloves pretended to open a door and invited some passers-by inside. But since then it's stepped up an invisible staircase to new heights, and is now the world's longest-running and most influential visual theatre festival. It draws 16,000 mime fans and their very real money every year.

SLOANE ARRANGER

An old house in London's Great Russell Street opened its doors today in 1759 and forever changed the world of antiquities and academia. Inside were the artefacts and library owned by London physician and famous collector Sir Hans Sloane (yes, as in Sloane Square). This was the genesis of a revolutionary institution that would be owned by the nation, free to all, and would collect everything – the British Museum. It now has more than seven million objects and is one of the world's most comprehensive records of human culture. Curiously, the first choice of venue, Buckingham Palace, was rejected for its unsuitable location.

A HAT TO GO GAGA FOR

Forget Lady Gaga's telephone hat and other outlandish headpieces – the original bonnet bandit was John Hetherington, a London haberdasher. When he strolled out today in 1797 wearing the world's first top hat he was arraigned before the Lord Mayor of London on a charge of breach of the peace and inciting a riot. Officers stated that 'several women fainted at the unusual sight, while children screamed and dogs yelped'.

AH'M 'AVIN' BARNEY RUBBLE WITH ME CHALFONT ST GILES

Every major city has its patois, but few are as much of a bubble bath as Cockney Rhyming Slang. It has been amusing locals and confusing tourists since the 1840s and was first officially recognised in *A Dictionary of Modern Slang, Cant, and Vulgar Words* by John Camden Hotten (published today in 1859). Much of it is wildly obscure, but it's fun when some really juicy words enter the mainstream: few users of the mild 'berk' know which rhyme it originally derived from.

JOLLY HOCKEY STICKS

As long as there have been sticks and stones, people have probably played some sort of hockey. Quite a long time then. But the modern game bullied off in London, with the first club being founded at Blackheath and the rules coming from a version of the sport played by Middlesex cricket clubs over the winter. The official governing body, The Hockey Association, was formed today in 1886. Alas, the nation's schoolboys had to wait a few more years before an indecently short hockey skirt was invented.

CAN YOU TELL ME HOW TO GET TO STANFORDS?

Need a walking map of Norway? A guide to the Moscow metro? A chart of the journey tea makes? How about a Christmas bauble painted as a globe? If it's map-related, Stanfords on Long Acre is the place to get it. This is the world's largest map retailer, by far, and was established today in 1853 by Edward Stanford. Dozens of intrepid travellers have come here for their maps before getting lost in the wilds, including Florence Nightingale, Amy Johnson, David Livingstone, Captain Robert Falcon Scott, Ernest Shackleton and Michael Palin.

THE MARLBOROUGH MAN

What could be more American than the Marlboro Man, that virile symbol of the world's most popular cigarette? Well, this mega-brand is *actually* named after Great Marlborough Street in Soho. Philip Morris was a tobacconist from Whitechapel who set up a factory in what was at one time a street of the aristocracy; his firm expanded to New York in 1902. The brand was first sold today in 1924 with its name simplified to avoid confusing Americans.

EGGS-TRAORDINARY EDIBLES

Le Boulestin was London's most expensive restaurant in the 1930s, and its owner Marcel Boulestin was the Gordon Ramsay of his day. If a little less grumpy. This French-born foodie became the world's first ever television chef today in 1937 when he presented the BBC series *Cook's Night Out*. And what did this genius gastronome show the great British public how to cook? An omelette. Which is probably all they could handle, to be fair.

SPORT HITS THE AIRWAVES

The world's first ever live radio commentary on a football match was relayed from Highbury today in 1927, as Arsenal and Sheffield United drew 1–1. This was one week after the first ever rugby broadcast, also from London, of England v Wales at Twickenham. Highbury's tube station was renamed 'Arsenal' in 1932, making it the only station on the Underground to be named after a football club.

JOBBERS AND DRINKERS

Britain's very first specialist commercial building, the Royal Exchange, opened in the heart of the City today in 1571. Queen Elizabeth I bestowed its royal title and, more importantly, its licence to sell booze. Over the next four centuries, the Exchange became the beating heart of commerce in the capital, helping it become the world's primary business centre. Always keen to keep a clean reputation, the Exchange banned one group completely in the 17th century for their extremely rude manners – stockbrokers.

TODAY'S DAILY GOOD TURN

In the Boer War, many young lads did a terrific job as scouts and messengers. Lieutenant General Robert Baden-Powell (from Paddington) was so impressed with their resourcefulness and initiative that he decided to introduce it to civilian life on his return to England. Today in 1908 he published a book, *Scouting For Boys*, that would sell 100 million copies and launch a whole new youth pursuit. Over 28 million people worldwide enjoy scouting, making it one of our most enduring exports.

DID I FORGET TO SAY I INVENTED PHOTOGRAPHY?

When French artist Louis Daguerre claimed to have taken the world's first fixed photographic images, William Henry Fox Talbot piped up and pointed out that he'd been happily snapping for over four years. He showed these historic shots at London's Royal Institution today in 1839. Talbot's 'Calotype' negatives could be reproduced multiple times as positives, unlike 'Daguerrotypes', and his negative/positive process became the basis for almost all 19th- and 20th-century photography. If only he'd chosen a more interesting subject for his early images than the streets of Reading.

A BETTER CLASS OF SNACK

The Piccadilly super-pantry Fortnum & Mason is an English institution (founded in St James today in 1707), but it's not just for Londoners too posh to go to Tesco. The store invented that staple of our motorway service stations, the Scotch egg – over two centuries before Ginsters got anywhere near our English arteries. Back then Piccadilly was the Heston services of its day, full of coaching inns for travellers heading out of town, and a hand-sized, meaty-egg snack was just the thing to pick up for the journey. F&M was also the first shop in England to take a chance on stocking Heinz baked beans – they were an expensive imported delicacy in the 1930s.

SHE'S MY TOWER OF STRENGTH

Thomas Rich was a baker's apprentice from Ludgate Hill who fell in love with his employer's daughter and asked her to marry him. Wanting to make a good impression with his father-in-law, he decided to create a wedding cake that would top all others. Looking around for inspiration today in 1703, he saw the round, tiered spire of nearby St Bride's Church. And so he produced a confection just like it (although without a vicar inside) – the first modern tiered wedding cake.

CITY LIGHTS

The historical picture of London might be of a dark and dingy metropolis, but really it has been the world's best-lit city for centuries. Illumination in London's public streets was ordered as long ago as 1417 by Sir Henry Barton, the Mayor of London. Rotten Row in Hyde Park was the first street to be fully artificially lit when it was illuminated with oil lamps in 1690. And the first public street lighting with gas was lit in Pall Mall today in 1807.

NO, IT DOESN'T HAVE A KFC

Just a teensy bit more exclusive than Bluewater, Burlington Arcade off Piccadilly was the world's first shopping centre. Lord George Cavendish, who lived in what is now the Royal Academy next door, wanted to stop passing ruffians from chucking rubbish, especially their empty oyster shells, over his garden wall, so he built a promenade of shops in 1819. Security is still enforced by the formidable Beadles in traditional top hats and frock coats. Gladstone Collars were created here, and Hancocks the jewellers have made every Victoria Cross since the award was created, today in 1856.

FOYLED AGAIN

With 30 miles (48.3km) of shelving, Foyles on the Charing Cross Road (opened today in 1906) was for a long time the world's largest bookshop. It was also the most eccentric, with a layout apparently designed by an Edwardian maniac. Books were categorised by publisher, rather than by topic or author. Buying a volume meant queuing three times: to collect an invoice, to pay the invoice and to collect the book (because sales staff weren't allowed to handle cash). It was so labyrinthine that the untrained staff barely knew which floor they were on, let alone where your book was.

A BIG CLAP FOR THE NEW HOSPITAL

The fact that London opened the world's first specialist venereal and tropical disease clinic is a medical advance to be proud of. That it was to deal with the problem of London being the syphilis capital of the world in the 16th and 17th centuries – not so much. Thanks to all those adventurers in their fancy ships sailing to parts unknown and bringing back God-knows-what in their breeches, the London Lock Hospital was opened in Grosvenor Place on this day in 1747. Its name came from the 'locks', or rags that lepers used to wear. Nice.

FEBRUARY

YOU CAN'T PARK THERE

London is the world's greenest city – wait, what are you laughing at? I'm serious. Almost 40 per cent of Greater London – 67 square miles (173km²) – is green space, more than any other city its size. For that we can thank King Henry VIII: he seized vast amounts of land from the church after dissolving the monasteries (beginning today in 1535) and set up large Royal Parks. There are eight of these in London, adding 8 square miles (20.7km²) of green space. Not that Henry did this for us proles – the parks were hunting grounds for his royal cronies. Even today the public has no legal right to use the Parks, and having a sarnie by the Serpentine depends entirely on the grace and favour of The Crown.

RELIEVING CITY CONGESTION

It was great news for beer-loving journalists today in 1852 – the world's first modern public conveniences opened in Fleet Street. They were established, somewhat incongruously, by the Society of Arts. And, this being Victorian England, they were called 'Public Waiting Rooms', and the loos for men and women were on opposite sides of the street. Users were charged a standard fee of 1d, which is how the phrase 'to spend a penny' was coined.

DON'T YOU DARE GIVE US A TWIRL

The Windmill Theatre was a Soho sensation thanks to its nude 'tableaux vivants' – girls with their kit off – which started today in 1932. This was only possible because the owner pointed out to the censor that as nude statues are allowed on the streets, if the girls stood still on stage they couldn't be obscene either. The censor had to agree (plus, he probably had tickets for later) and ruled: 'If you move, it's rude.' The Windmill was also where many famous comedians got their big breaks, including Tony Hancock, Harry Secombe, Peter Sellers, Michael Bentine, Barry Cryer, Tommy Cooper and Bruce Forsyth. Thank goodness they weren't doing the posing.

LIGHTS, CAMERA ... LONDON!

4 London is now the world's third busiest movie-making city, after LA and New York. It has three big studios: Shepperton, Leavesden and Pinewood, which was transformed from a sleepy Victorian country house into one of the world's most successful film factories. Its very first film was the fittingly titled *London Melody*, released today in 1937. Classics shot there include *Harry Potter*, the *Carry On* series, *Batman*, *Superman*, *Bourne* and, of course, most of the 23 James Bond adventures.

THE ORIGINAL MAD MAN

5 The *London Gazette* is the oldest English newspaper and the world's oldest surviving journal, first appearing today in 1666. Although its longevity isn't due to it being an exciting read – the *Gazette* is an official Government journal of record, in which statutory notices must be published. Definitely no Page 3 girls. It's also notable because in 1812 one of its officers, George Reynell, established the world's first advertising agency.

THE MAGIC ROUNDABOUT

6

East London Tech City, or Silicon Roundabout, is the largest technology start-up cluster in Europe and the third largest in the world after San Francisco and New York. In 2008, this area around the Old Street roundabout had 15 media and high-tech companies, two years later there were 85; while a report published today in 2012 counted 5,000 such firms. And that incredible growth comes *despite* David Cameron getting behind the area's development. With all these hip commuters it's no surprise the Roundabout is also the country's top location for headphone-wearing cyclists getting knocked off their single-speed bikes.

SCIENCE IS BLOODY AMAZING

7

Next time you arrive at work with some mysterious itches on your body, be proud, not annoyed – you've just been bitten by an utterly unique species of mosquito. This charming little insect has evolved to live underground in the dark in the Tube system, where it feeds on the blood of the half million mice and three million commuters who share its living space daily. Biologists, giddy at discovering this living example of evolution in action, named it *Culex pipiens molestus* (today in 2001) after its particularly vicious bite.

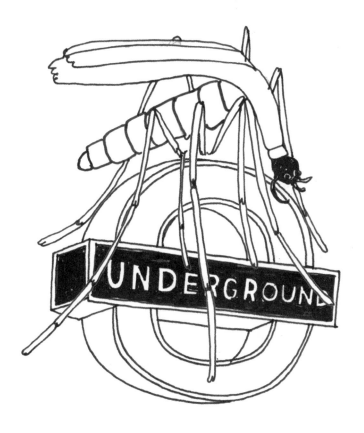

A MONUMENTAL MEMORIAL

The Monument is the world's tallest free-standing stone column and the world's least imaginatively named monument. Opened today in 1677, it commemorates the Great Fire of London, which destroyed 80 per cent of the city in 1666, including St Paul's cathedral and 87 churches. It's a Doric column 202ft (62m) high, and is sited the same distance from the source of the fire, at Farynor's bakery in Pudding Lane. This is very nearly where the Roman bridge reached the north bank: perhaps the true birthplace of London itself.

PETER'S GREAT IDEA

Deptford has a very unlikely son – Peter the Great. For it was here that the 26-year-old Tsar Peter I of Russia came in 1698 to study the latest shipbuilding technology. Peter was welcomed by King William III and billeted at the home of the writer John Evelyn on this day. During a four-month residence Peter visited the Royal Observatory, Society and Dockyards and learned enough to later build the Russian navy and become a dazzlingly successful tyrant. While in London though, he apparently spent much of his time getting wrecked with his mates and pushing each other through Evelyn's hedge in a wheelbarrow.

CHAPTER ONE FOR
THE BESTSELLING AUTHOR

10 What is the bestselling novel ever, in any language? Thankfully it's not *50 Shades*, but *A Tale Of Two Cities*, by Charles Dickens (200 million copies sold). Dickens created some of the most memorable characters in literary history, including Oliver Twist, Ebenezer Scrooge, Mr Micawber, Miss Havisham and Uriah Heep. 'Dickensian London' has entered our imagination as a real place – not that you'd like to go there. And it was today in 1836 that Dickens' first novel, *The Pickwick Papers*, was commissioned as a monthly serial. It was an immediate success, bringing the 24-year-old writer instant fame.

NO, WE THINK YOU'LL FIND THAT
TOYS ARE *US*

11 Hamleys is the oldest, largest and most awesome toy shop in the world. It was founded by William Hamley, who opened his 'Noah's Ark' toy shop at No. 231 High Holborn in London in 1760. Today's flagship store on Regent Street has seven floors of wonders and celebrated its 250th birthday today in 2010. Hamleys was bombed five times in the Blitz, presumably because the Germans didn't want London's youth fighting back with catapults.

GOING CLUBBING, SIR MONTY?

12

London has more clubs than any other city in the world, although the craziest thing you can do in them is order a double G&T – yes, we mean gentlemen's clubs. The nook of Pall Mall and St James's Street is stuffed with these stuffed shirt repositories, the oldest and most prestigious being White's. This first opened its doors today in 1693 as a hot chocolate emporium called Mrs White's Chocolate House, run by an Italian immigrant. David Cameron resigned from White's in 2008 because of the club's refusal to admit female members – either that, or because they wouldn't stock his favourite marshmallows.

AS HONEST AS THEIR BONUSES ARE LARGE

13

Considering it was aimed at 'The Honest Financier and the Respectable Broker', you might think the *Financial Times* would have struggled to find a market when it was first published today in London in 1888. But somehow it did, and its salmon-pink pages are now perused by half a million honest and respectable (at least in their own eyes) readers every working day. It is still the world's most influential business publication.

ABRAHAM'S MIGHTY SWELLING ORGAN

The organ in the church of St Magnus the Martyr in Pudding Lane first honked out a hymn of praise today in 1712. In doing so it revolutionised the design of that most magnificent of instruments. Created by famous organ builder Abraham Jordan, it was the first organ in the world to feature a swell-box. This set of enclosed pipes allowed a player to control the organ's volume like never before. Now known as the 'expression pedal', it's standard on organs, electronic keyboards and guitars.

LOVE IS IN THE AIR

The statue of Eros, the Greek god of love, in Piccadilly Circus is a world famous and beautiful symbol of London. Except it isn't Eros at all, but his brother Anteros, god of requited love. The statue was dedicated today in 1893 as a monument to the Earl of Shaftesbury. The earl was a pioneering social reformer who helped stop small boys being used as chimney sweeps. Whatever you want to call his sculpture, it was the first in the world to be made out of aluminium.

I HEARD IT ON THE GREAT VINE

It's fair to say that London is usually regarded as a wine-glugging, rather than a wine-growing place. But in a conservatory at Hampton Court Palace is the world's largest vine. The 'Great Vine' was planted by superstar landscape gardener Lancelot 'Capability' Brown today in 1769. He picked a good spot, because by 1887 the vine was 4ft (1.2m) around the base – today it's 12ft (3.7m) round and over 100ft (30.5m) long. It produces around 600lb (272kg) of juicy black grapes every year, although in 2001 it surpassed itself with a whopping crop of 845lb (383kg).

EVEN THEIR CARS HAVE DIPLOMATIC IMMUNITY

From a personal point of view the London Congestion Charge (introduced today in 2003) is a pain in the backside – and the wallet. But looking at the bigger picture it has actually been one of the world's most successful such ventures. It has lowered accidents and emissions, and raised around £90 million a year to help fund Mayor Boris Johnson's other brilliant (or crackpot, depending on your point of view) schemes. Curiously, the US Embassy has refused ever to pay the charge, racking up £3.44 million of unpaid bills to date.

WILD WILD EAST

18 London's docklands were once home to the largest pet shop the world has ever seen – Jamrach's Animal Emporium near Tobacco Dock. The owner, Charles Jamrach, opened a vast menagerie (today in 1840) of every stripe of exotic animal, which he sold to circus owners, collectors and noblemen who fancied walking a leopard around Mayfair. The world's busiest port thronged with sailors who knew they could sell Jamrach every odd beast they sneaked back from wild places. Today, a statue of a small boy facing a large escaped tiger commemorates a notable, if inevitable, event in the shop's history.

DA-NA-NA-NA-NA-NAA-NAAAAAA

It's the show that introduced the world to the splendours of London's East End. First broadcast today in 1985, *EastEnders* is Britain's most depressing – sorry, successful – drama programme, regularly topping the viewing figures. Famous for its realism and broaching taboo issues with mainstream audiences, this slice of London life is popular worldwide but is watched most keenly by the control staff of the National Grid. When the credits roll the power demand surges by three gigawatts, the equivalent of 1.75 million kettles being flipped on.

PHYLLIS FINDS A WAY

20 Phyllis Pearsall was heading to a dinner party in London tonight in 1935 when she got lost. The most recent city map was 17 years old; useless, considering that the suburbs had almost doubled in size in those years. Nine thousand streets simply weren't on the map. In a move many might consider extreme, Phyllis began waking up at 5am every day, walking solidly for 18 hours to check the names of the 23,000 streets of London. She walked 3,000 miles (4,828km) and in 1936 had created the world's first comprehensive city A-Z. Amazingly, no publisher would accept it, so she printed it herself and founded Geographers' A-Z Map Company, still going strong today.

DRINKERS OF THE WORLD, UNITE!

21 It's odd that the greatest critics of our society have suckled at its breast. Karl Marx wrote *Das Kapital* in the British Museum, while cadging money off Friedrich Engels and getting pissed, and the pair wrote *The Communist Manifesto* (published today in 1848) in a room above the Red Lion pub on Great Windmill Street. Vladimir Lenin and Josef Stalin quaffed ale together at the Crown in Clerkenwell, and it was here that Stalin first fell out with Leon Trotsky. Mahatma Gandhi studied law at Inner Temple and

Ho Chi Minh lived in Crouch End. Oh, and Alois Hitler, Adolf's half-brother, also hung out here – before moving to Liverpool.

QUEEN OF ALL THE COMMUTERS

A female English Braveheart – that's a handy way to imagine the warrior Queen Boudicca. She led a major uprising of the Iceni tribe against the occupying Roman forces in 60 AD. And today in 1988 archaeologists found what they think might have been her grave right here in London – under platform 8 at King's Cross station, in fact. Of course, it might just have been a commuter still waiting for the six o'clock to Peterborough, but it's a nice story.

SINGLE-SPEED PENNY FARTHING FOR SALE

Technology really is a marvellous thing – before eBay we had to buy and sell our useless tat via a newspaper. For over a century the classified adverts published in the back pages were the only place to go if you needed a wobbly bunk bed or a one-eyed kitten. And this whole concept originated in London, when the first such advertisement appeared today in 1886 in the pages of *The Times*. Mind you, the guy who placed it got annoyed with all the time-wasting postcards he received.

BRILLIANT BOOZERS

If there's one thing that London does better than any other city on Earth, it's pubs. From quirky old City taverns to Hampstead coaching inns, and even Shoreditch bars full of young trendies, we've got the lot. One of the oldest is the Spaniards Inn (established today in 1585), frequented by Dick Turpin, Charles Dickens and Dracula. In the early 14th century, London's 354 taverns served a population of 45,000 – one for every 127 citizens. Today our eight million citizens only have 7,000 pubs – one for every 1,142 drinkers. We need *more* pubs!

POLLY WOULD LIKE A CRACKER

Pigeons? Pah, every city in Europe has pigeons, but only London has parakeets. There are at least 30,000 green ring-necked parakeets living in the southeast, with large colonies brightening up Hampton Court, Kew Gardens, Croydon and even Esher Rugby Club. They're descended from extras who escaped from the Isleworth Studios set of the Humphrey Bogart movie *The African Queen*, today in 1951. Although another tale insists that Jimi Hendrix released a pair into the skies above Carnaby Street in the 1960s and they promptly got experienced. Now if Ed Sheeran could release some condors in Camden …

TO RUSSIA, WITH GLOVES

The Muscovy Company, organised by a group of London merchants and chartered today in 1555, was the world's very first joint stock company. Their traders hooked up with Tsar Ivan IV, securing a monopoly on the import of huge amounts of Russian furs, timber, whale oil and wax. Their vessels shipped English clothes and textiles the other way. The Company is still going today, although it mostly does charitable work, rather than importing polar bear skins into Shadwell.

A CHANGE OF DIRECTION

Maps should be geographically correct, right? Well, so people thought when drawing the first Tube maps. But the central stations were crammed together, suburban ones were miles apart, and the lines swirled all over the place. Then Leyton-born draughtsman Harry Beck realised that travellers only needed to know the order of stations and where to change. Throwing spatial correctness out of the window he simplified the lines into verticals, horizontals and diagonals with his revolutionary Underground map published today in 1933. London got a new icon and the world got a design classic. Harry got 5 guineas.

DEAD POETS' SOCIETY

You'll find the world's most talented collection of ghosts in Westminster Abbey. That's because in a section of the south transept is Poets' Corner, where more literary legends are buried than anywhere else in the world. First in was Geoffrey Chaucer, who died in 1400 but took up residence today in 1556. Edmund Spenser was next, with Samuel Johnson, Charles Dickens, John Dryden, Thomas Hardy, Rudyard Kipling, Richard Sheridan and Alfred Tennyson all following. William Shakespeare has a memorial there – near where Laurence Olivier lies, who fittingly played so many of the bard's great characters.

MARCH

CAN A COW'S BUM BE ART?

If it was on an album cover designed by Hipgnosis, absolutely. This legendary London design team did just that with Pink Floyd's *Atom Heart Mother*, before creating the iconic prism-on-black of *The Dark Side of the Moon* (released today in 1973). This sealed their high-selling reputation and they created cover art for everyone who was anyone in Rock: Led Zeppelin, T. Rex, 10cc, Wings, AC/DC, Genesis, Yes, Black Sabbath and ELO. Hipgnosis didn't bill their clients, instead asking that they pay 'what they thought the cover was worth'. God bless the '70s ...

TABARD CENTRAL

Many City workers walk past a set of dusty brick buildings on Queen Victoria Street without knowing how historic they really are. The College of Arms was founded today in 1484 by charter from King Richard III, and it's the oldest heraldic college in the world. If you've ever wondered who sorts out all the flags, shields and trumpets for a coronation or royal wedding – now you know. The College also conducts genealogical research, and if you fancy getting a family coat of arms they'll happily draw one up. Although such a heraldic logo will set you back the royal sum of £4,400.

FASHION FIRST

Some alarmingly dressed youths strutted about a west London car park today in 1984 and rather than get arrested they started something amazing – London Fashion Week. There were catwalk classics by Ghost and Zandra Rhodes as well as John Galliano's show-stopping debut collection. Now the event is one of the 'Big Four', alongside New York, Paris and Milan fashion weeks, drawing 5,000 press and buyers to Somerset House and pulling in orders of £100 million. Unlike many other week-long festivals, there isn't much call for burger stands.

ALL-ROUND ALL-STAR

C.B. Fry from Croydon was the most gifted all-round sportsman ever. Fry was England cricket captain, scoring 30,000 first-class runs at an average of over 50, and still holds the record for most consecutive first-class centuries – six, which he set in 1901. He represented England at football and played in the FA Cup Final for Southampton F.C. At Oxford he got 12 sporting blues, while today in 1893 he equalled the world record for the long jump, leaping 23ft 6½in (7.17m). Fry was a talented author, academic and diplomat who also turned down the throne of Albania. His party trick was to leap backwards from a standing position onto the mantelpiece, a feat he continued to do in his seventies.

WHEELY GOOD NEWS

The older Tube stations might be a nightmare for wheelchair users, but modern transport is adapting – London has the largest accessible bus fleet in the world. There are 8,500 London buses on 700 routes, carrying 2.3 billion passengers a year, and they are all wheelchair accessible (as announced in the Mayor's transport plan today in 2012). So too are all 22,000 black cabs. However, much of the time you can wheel yourself in a chair faster than a bus can get through rush hour traffic.

ANYONE SEEN SIR ALEC'S CLOAK?

Angels & Bermans isn't a second-rate Dan Brown, but the world's oldest entertainment costume supplier. Opened in 1840 by Morris Angel in Seven Dials, it was a second-hand clothing shop, until an actor asked if he could rent a suit rather than buy it. Angel agreed and went on to corner the market. Their outfits have appeared in 33 films that have won Best Costume Oscars, including *Titanic*, *Lawrence of Arabia* and *Star Wars*. Obi-Wan Kenobi's original cloak was rediscovered hanging on the rails in 2005 – it had been rented to the public as a monk's cloak for 28 years. Today in 2007 it sold for £55,000.

THE BUZZ OF LEARNING

Ten chemical elements, 15 Nobel prizes and the electrical generator – all came from the Royal Institution, formed today in 1799 in Soho Square. It had the specific purpose of 'diffusing knowledge', and the Institution soon became world famous under the guidance of early members Humphry Davy and Michael Faraday. The Institution's Christmas Lectures have set thousands of young scientists on the road to discovery. Perhaps most importantly of all, one of its founders, Count Rumford, invented the percolating coffee pot.

BRIGHT THINKING

The world's largest solar-powered bridge was completed today in 2013 at Blackfriars. Before you panic, it doesn't use the London sun to keep the tracks up – we'd be in trouble then. Instead it uses the electricity generated by 4,400 photovoltaic panels to power Blackfriars station. This cuts the station's carbon emissions by 511 tons a year. Now if we could only work out how to power Charing Cross by drizzle, we'd be laughing.

THE EYE IN THE SKY

The London Eye was the largest Ferris wheel in the world when it opened today in 2000, standing 443ft (135m) above the Thames. This famous landmark has 32 passenger pods (33 really, but pod 13 is always empty), representing London's 32 boroughs. Every year, nearly four million people step aboard to enjoy a pigeon's-eye view of the capital. Taller wheels have since been built, but none with the Eye's one-sided support frame. The marketers cling to this fact to bill it as 'the world's tallest cantilevered observation wheel'. Catchy.

MEGA-CITY ONE

When Great Britain's first complete census was taken on this rainy Tuesday back in 1801, it showed that London was the world's first industrialised city to have a population of over a million: 1,011,157 to be precise. In the whole nation there were 10.9 million people living in 1.8 million houses. Our capital would hold the official title of greatest city on Earth for over a century, until it was overtaken by New York in 1925. London's population had then ballooned to 7,419,000.

STREET OF SHAME

No newspapers are actually published in Fleet Street any more, but this was once such a hotspot of high-quality journalism that the name lives on as a general term for the industry. The area had a few book publishers in the 16th century and then, today in 1702, Edward Mallet printed the *Daily Courant*, London's first daily newspaper, from premises above the White Hart Inn. By the early 19th century, there were 52 London papers, 100 other titles and Fleet Street was famous as the world's newspaper nerve centre. Or should that be infamous?

TOP FOR TOWPATHS

Little Venice should be renamed Massive Venice – that's because London has more miles of canal than the watery Italian city. Almost four times as many, in fact, with 100 miles of capital canal versus a measly 26 in Venice. The first proper canal in London was the Limehouse Cut, which connected the Lea Navigation and the Thames. Barges began using it today in 1769. London used to have even more waterways, with the Grand Surrey Canal, Croydon Canal, Kensington Canal and Grosvenor Canal all disappearing over the years. Venice does have more gondolas, though.

ANIMAL MAGIC

London Zoo is the world's oldest scientific zoo, established in 1828. It was originally a private collection of animals for scientists to study. But in 1847 the Fellows realised that they could charge punters for the privilege of peering at their possums, and the zoo was opened to the general public on this day. Its reptile house (1849), aquarium (1853) and insect house (1881) were also the first in the world, as was its children's zoo (1938). Although, disappointingly, children weren't actually put in cages.

THE QUEEN OF LONDON STATIONS

'What palace is that?' we have heard while walking along the Euston Road, and happily pointed out it's actually a railway terminus. St Pancras really is the most splendid station, which the Midland Railway expressly wanted when it commissioned architect George Gilbert Scott to create the biggest and most spectacular hotel in the city. Amazingly, only poet John Betjeman's campaign stopped it being demolished in the 1960s. After decades of dereliction the spruced-up hotel reopened to guests today in 2011, 138 years after its first incarnation. Shall we celebrate in the world's longest Champagne bar?

IT'S A BIT WILD ROUND HERE, INNIT?

Eighteen thousand years ago London's East End was a cold, harsh land where wild hairy creatures roamed around roaring at each other and fighting viciously. Yep, exactly. In fact, the Roding Valley area is one of Europe's premier mega-fauna fossil sites. Tiger, wolf, bear, elephant, rhinoceros, bison and hippopotamus have all been dug up here, and the only complete mammoth skull ever discovered in Britain was unearthed today in 1860, where Boots the Chemist now stands in Ilford High Road. Woolly rhinos have also been found beneath Trafalgar Square.

THAMESIDE TEMPLE OF POWER

Despite now being little more than a shell, Battersea Power Station is still the largest brick building in Europe. It's famous for its four leg-like chimneys, but for much of its existence it only had two – the station was built in identical halves, 20 years apart. It's now held in affection as one of the city's great landmarks, but when construction began today in 1929 there were huge protests about it being an eyesore. So the builders commissioned famous architect Sir Giles Gilbert Scott, designer of Liverpool Anglican Cathedral and the classic red telephone box, to create something a bit special.

BIRTH CONTROL BREAKTHROUGH

The 1918 book *Married Love* was condemned as obscene – not because it was a raunchy novel, but because it had the audacity to educate women about birth control. Written by UCL academic Marie Stopes, it proved so popular it was in its sixth printing within a fortnight. At 25, Stopes became the youngest person ever to earn a D.Sc. She later opened the Mothers' Clinic in Holloway today in 1921, Britain's first clinic to offer women birth control advice. Stopes played a major role in promoting reproductive health and breaking down taboos about sex.

DEEP COVER

18 Should the bomb ever drop, you can be proud that London will keep on running. Well, the capital's most powerful people won't die, anyway. That's because London has the most extensive underground military citadels of any city. The Cabinet War Rooms once extended 3 acres (1.2ha) underground, housing 528 people with a canteen, hospital and shooting range. There's a facility under Whitehall with the awesome Bond-like codename of Q-Whitehall, and the Admiralty Citadel is linked by tunnels to government buildings. But the king of catacombs is PINDAR, a bunker below the Ministry of Defence that's so extensive it cost £126.3 million and took ten years to build, finally opening today in 1994.

BOOT AND BUN

Sloane Rangers, pensioners, ludicrous football ticket prices – Chelsea has given so much to the world. It also produced the Chelsea boot, patented by Queen Victoria's shoemaker J. Sparkes-Hall today in 1851 (apparently she seldom wore anything else as she ruled a quarter of the planet). But surely the area's most wonderful export is the Chelsea bun. This delicacy was first created in the 18th century at the Bun House by Grosvenor Row, where the buns were so good they drew hungry Hanoverian royalty. Bun fans of the lower orders also came flocking – on Good Friday in 1839 the Bun House sold almost a quarter of a million buns.

PC PICKLES

When the coveted Jules Rimet trophy, on display in Britain for the upcoming World Cup finals, was stolen from Westminster Central Hall today in 1966, the world was shocked. The police drew a blank. But then up stepped Pickles, a black and white collie. This noble hound was out walking his pet, David Corbett, today in South Norwood when he sniffed an interesting parcel jammed under a hedge. Pickles had just sniffed out the stolen golden trophy. England went on to win the tournament for the first and only time. Pickles, sadly, died choking on his lead while chasing a cat.

DOING WITHOUT DRIVERS

Today in 1963 saw the introduction of a whole new generation of computer-controlled trains to the London Underground. These technological marvels led the world in their capabilities: they didn't need a driver to start, accelerate or to brake. They did, however, still require an operator on board for safety reasons and to bellow 'Mind the gap!' repetitively at each and every station.

FOR GOD'S SAKE DON'T LOSE
LIECHTENSTEIN

The world's first jigsaw puzzle was created by cartographer John Spilsbury in his studio in Russell Court off Drury Lane today in 1766. Spilsbury placed a map of the world on thin board and cut along the borders of countries to create pieces – his puzzle was a teaching aid to help children learn geography. And for 20 years all jigsaws were dissected maps like Spilsbury's, until some fiend had the idea of doing a 10,000-piece picture of the Norfolk Broads.

A MAUVER AND A SHAKER IN THE CHEMISTRY WORLD

23 Before 1856, all dyes for colouring cloth were natural substances, expensive to make and easily washed out. Purple, an aristocratic colour since antiquity, was particularly hard to make – the process involved doing lengthy and unpleasant things to molluscs. Then on this day, chemist William Perkin was trying to make artificial quinine in his attic laboratory in Cable Street, Stepney, when he instead invented mauve, the first-ever aniline dye. This spawned the whole synthetic dye industry and launched organic chemistry as we know it today. Oh, and Perkin was only 18 at the time.

GOING FOR A JUMP ON THE HEATH

24 You can see many strange things on Hampstead Heath, depending on what time you go there, but none as strange as ski jumping. However, on this sunny spring day in 1950, crowds thrilled to witness perhaps the most incongruous sporting spectacle ever. London's greenest space was covered with 60 tons of snow flown in from Norway and an 80ft (24.4m) tower and take-off ramp were built. Then some bold, but rather unskilled, jumpers from Oxford and Cambridge Universities fell off the end before some Norwegians showed them how it should be done.

CAPTAIN FANTASTIC

Captain Thomas Coram was a shipbuilder and merchant who became dismayed at the number of abandoned babies he saw in London. So he set up the Foundling Hospital, which took in its first children today in 1741. It was the world's first incorporated charity. The original hospital in central London was demolished in the 1920s, but its site has since been turned into a children's play area, known as Coram's Fields.

BIRTH OF THE BOOK BUSINESS

Perhaps the first bestseller in British history, William Caxton's translation of *Aesop's Fables*, was lifted off his presses in Westminster today in 1484. Caxton learned his trade in Bruges, and later became the owner of the first printing press in England, translating and publishing over 100 classic books, including *The Canterbury Tales* and *Le Morte d'Arthur*. The fact that he printed so many in English means that he did more than anyone else to standardise what is now the world's number one international language, and our own mother tongue.

FLYING HIGH

Next time you take a BA flight at Heathrow, take pride for a moment in the majestic Terminal 5. For this is the largest free-standing structure in the United Kingdom. Five football pitches could fit on its roof (although the balls might roll off) and inside it has the longest escalator in Europe. Mind you, they had time to get it right. It took 19 years from conception to its opening today in 2008, including a four-year public inquiry – the longest in British history. Impressive, huh?

MERLIN GETS HIS SKATES ON

The world's very first pair of practical roller skates appeared today in 1760. John Joseph Merlin, a musician and inventor of Hanover Square, made a memorable entrance at a masquerade party, rolling in on metal-wheeled boots while playing the violin. Alas, he hadn't invented a way to stop or even manoeuvre them, and so crashed into a mirror. Still, he was far ahead of his time – Regent's Park hadn't been laid out yet, so there was nowhere for him to annoy people trying to have a quiet walk.

THE CLASSIC CLASSICAL VENUE

From the Proms to Pink Floyd, sumo wrestlers to school orchestras, the world's top performers in all artistic fields have graced the stage of London's Royal Albert Hall. One of the most recognisable buildings in the world, it was opened by Queen Victoria today in 1871 as a spectacular memorial to her deceased husband. Its huge arena can seat 5,272 people. Unfortunately, the Hall was so vast and impressive that it had a distinct echo. It was 'the only place where a British composer could be sure of hearing his work twice'.

THE SHARD STANDS PROUD (AND TALL)

Our wonderful Shard is the European Union's tallest building, and easily the world's pointiest. Officially the London Bridge Tower, it was topped out today in 2012 at a head-spinning 1,004ft (306m) high with 72 habitable floors. Filled with offices, restaurants and very rich tenants who don't get vertigo, it is also proving itself as a leisure destination. No sooner was it built than it was being leapt off by BASE jumpers, scaled by Greenpeace activists and dangled from by Prince Andrew.

RIVER CITY

London probably has more secret rivers than any other city, with at least 21 underground streams feeding the Thames. These were once used for transport and water, but as the city grew they became foul sewage-ditches that were best hidden underground. The river Fleet – yes, as in Fleet Street – was a major river, with a wide estuary and the oldest tidal mill in the world. It was finally covered over today in 1769. The Tyburn runs directly beneath Buckingham Palace, the Walbrook runs under Cannon Street and next time you're at Sloane Square Tube station look up – inside that metal tube is the Westbourne River.

APRIL

CLOCKS AWAY!

1 It's one of the world's most famous landmarks, and an essential bit of stock footage for every Hollywood movie that cuts to 'London, England' – the Elizabeth Tower by Parliament (Big Ben is the bell inside). Proudly standing 315ft (96m) high, the Tower features the largest four-faced chiming clock in the world, whose hour and minute hands are 9 and 14ft (2.7 and 4.3m) long respectively. But it isn't the largest clock in London. That honour goes to the clock on Shell Mex House at 80 Strand, which is 25ft (7.6m) in diameter and was known for many years as 'Big Benzene'. This address was where the Royal Air Force was formed today in 1918.

AN AWFULLY BIG ADVENTURE

One of London's favourite statues is that of the boy who never grew up, Peter Pan, which stands in Kensington Gardens. The statue's story is also one of the city's most heart-warming. *Peter Pan* was set in the Gardens and its author, J.M. Barrie, paid workmen to secretly erect the commemorative statue overnight. That way children would think it had arrived, like Tinkerbell, by magic. And today in 1929 the childless Barrie handed all copyright in the *Peter Pan* works over to Great Ormond Street Hospital, which to this day continues to profit from his gift.

LONDON CALLING

This was a big night in music history in 1976. Pub rock band The 101ers were headlining at the Nashville Room, but the lead singer was so blown away by the bold new music of his own support band that he promptly jacked The 101ers in and started a new group. The support band were the Sex Pistols, The 101ers' lead singer was Joe Strummer and his new outfit were The Clash. Punk had arrived and London was *the* place to be if you were a phlegm-spitting, safety-pin-wearing, anti-Christ anarchist.

TUNEFUL TRAVERSE

You took your life in your hands when you crossed the road before this day in 1949, because the few pedestrian crossings that existed were largely ignored by motorists. Then the first 1,000 zebra crossings were introduced, starting in London. They were so striking that motorists couldn't ignore them and had to stop. The most famous is the one featured on The Beatles' *Abbey Road* album, in north London – perhaps the only traffic safety feature that is also a cultural landmark. Curiously, the stripes were originally blue and yellow – not very zebra-like.

THESE GO UP TO 11 ...

In the early 1960s Jim Marshall was running a drum shop in west London when he started importing guitars and amps. His customers (who happened to include Eric Clapton, Jimi Hendrix and Pete Townshend) wanted a louder, more rocking sound, so he founded Marshall Amplification in 1964 to make the world's best amplifiers. When the musicians demanded even more oomph, Jim piled up the amps on top of each other, creating the speaker stack. Every year on this day, guitarists around the world post videos containing one minute of feedback, instead of silence, as a tribute to 'The Father of Loud', who died on 5 April 2012.

A STORE NOT TO BE SNIFFED AT

It's not just a London landmark: Harrods is the biggest shop in the UK by quite some distance. It covers 5 acres (2ha) – about three football pitches – and has over one million square feet (92,903m²) of selling space across 330 departments. Since it opened today back in 1824, it has become famous for selling everything you can think of at a price you'd rather not. Shame it's owned by Qatar, really. You could buy pure cocaine in Harrods until 1916, which probably helped you get your shopping done in good time.

THE KING OF SCIENCE-FICTION

Not many writers are influential enough to create an entire genre, but Bromley's own H.G. Wells was one of them. His first novel, *The Time Machine*, transported the field of science fiction into a new era, and he went on to write many more sci-fi classics, including *The Island of Doctor Moreau*, *The Invisible Man*, *The War of the Worlds* (published today in serialised form in 1897) and *The First Men in the Moon*. Before writing professionally, Wells was a teacher. One of his pupils was A.A. Milne, future creator of another English literary icon, Winnie-the-Pooh.

BEST IN SHOW

A dog-mad chap called Charles Cruft decided to hold a parade of pooches today in 1891 at the Royal Agricultural Hall, Islington. Not expecting many entries, he found out that we really are a nation of animal lovers when 2,437 dogs of 36 breeds arrived. His eponymous show is still going strong, with around 28,000 dogs entering Crufts each year, bringing 160,000 humans with them. It's the world's largest annual dog show, and the highlight of the year for poop-scoop manufacturers.

STICKING TWO FINGERS UP TO FASHION

Vivienne Westwood was a school teacher when she began selling clothes inspired by bikers, prostitutes and fetishists in Malcolm McLaren's 'SEX' boutique in the King's Road (established today in 1974). When the McLaren-managed band the Sex Pistols hit the charts, Westwood's punk and new wave fashions hit the mainstream. Westwood has since won British Fashion Designer of the Year three times, including in 2006 at the age of 65. Pharrell Williams' famous buffalo hat is a Westwood design.

COPYRIGHT ON

The piracy of creative works is nothing new. Before this day in 1710 the Stationers' Company (one of the Livery Companies of the City of London) had a monopoly on the printing trade. All books had to be entered on their register and only a Company member could do so; corruption, censorship and illegal copying were rife. Then the Statute of Anne introduced the world's first copyright legislation. Now publishers had 14 years' legal protection and the author was identified as the legal owner of the work.

SUCCESS IS IN THE POST FOR HIM

If you think queues at the post office are bad now, before today in 1855 you had to queue up every time you wanted even to post a single letter. Then a clerk from the post office at St Martin's-le-Grand gave the world a brilliant new way of collecting mail – the pillar box. London got its first five green boxes on this day – they weren't painted red until 1874. Good though this idea was, it wasn't the clerk's best: he wrote a novel that same year and became bestselling writer Anthony Trollope.

AN IDEA WORTH STICKING WITH

The world's first adhesive postage stamp, the Penny Black, was printed in London today in 1840. Which, considering yesterday's entry, is a classic case of things happening in the wrong order. Rowland Hill's idea had been poo-pooed by the Post Office at first, but it proved a winner with customers and within just a few weeks over 600,000 were being printed daily. And no wonder – before the Penny Black you paid more the further the letter went. Bad news if Granny lived in North Uist.

A MARATHON EFFORT

The London Marathon is the world's largest annual fund-raising event – not surprising, considering how many sponsorship emails land in our inboxes every spring. Over £450 million has been raised for charity since 1981, with a whopping £47.2 million in 2009 alone. The London course is also where the women's world record time of 2:15:25 was set, by Paula Radcliffe, today in 2003. More importantly, in 2009 it also saw the world record for the fastest run by someone dressed as a fruit – 4:32:28 by the excellently named Sally Orange.

APRIL

THE EMPIRE'S BIG BREAK

14 For nearly 200 years, the Royal Military Academy at Woolwich trained the officers who helped shape the British Empire – which at one point covered a quarter of the entire planet. From its establishment today in 1741 until it closed in 1939, the Academy was the factory for that indefatigable type of fighting Englishman, with a stiff upper lip and a never-say-die attitude. It also helped give the world the game of snooker – a former Academy cadet in India created the game in 1875.

GROOVY, BABY, GROOVY

15 London's rebirth from post-war austerity was complete today in 1966 when it was officially the coolest city on the planet. For that's when the term 'Swinging London' first hit the mainstream, appearing in the pages of *Time* magazine. This reflected a general trend of grooviness: British bands were rocking the world; Carnaby Street wasn't a tourist nightmare and was actually cool; artists and designers made the King's Road a hip place to be; Twiggy was the world's most famous model; England were about to win the World Cup; Michael Caine was Alfie; Connery was Bond; and Minis were everywhere.

THE TRAMP TRIUMPHS

It was 1896, and a seven-year-old boy whose mother had been locked up in a lunatic asylum and whose father was dying of alcoholism was grubbing for existence in the London poorhouse. By 1918, he was the most famous man on the planet. Charles Spencer Chaplin (born today in 1889) escaped from his ferociously poor start in life to succeed first in vaudeville and then on film. He wrote, directed, produced, edited, wrote the music, and starred in most of his movies. At 26 he was earning $670,000 a year, making him one of the highest-paid people in the world – a rags to riches tale too extreme for a cinema audience to believe!

PACK YOUR BAGS,
THIS IS GOING TO GET BAWDY

On this day in 1397, Geoffrey Chaucer told his *Canterbury Tales* for the first time, to the London court of Richard II. Chaucer's poetic epic isn't just one of the major early works in English and a world literary classic, it's also the genesis of a whole genre. The royal court revelled in the raucous tale of a motley crew of pilgrims taking to the road for Canterbury and telling tales en route. The fact that many of these feature debauchery, misadventure and violence no doubt kept the audience happy.

EWE ARE NOW FREE

The granting of the Freedom of the City of London is the world's oldest such ceremony, with the first Freedom presented today in 1237. It meant the recipient was not the property of a feudal lord but could earn money and own land. Later this became simply the right to trade in the Square Mile. Now it's a mark of general respect, earned by worthies as various as Admiral Nelson, David Livingstone, Florence Nightingale, Winston Churchill, Princess Diana, Annie Lennox and Stephen Fry. One of a Freeman's ancient privileges is the right to drive sheep over London Bridge, which Fry duly did in 2013.

A CURRENCY OF NOTE

The British pound is the world's oldest currency still in use – we've been spending them for 1,200 years. Back in 775 AD, the Anglo-Saxon King Offa introduced pennies of pure silver. By 1279 the Royal Mint was creating our coins in the Tower of London. The first fully printed banknotes were introduced today in 1853 by the Bank of England, in Threadneedle Street. Before then each note was numbered and signed by hand by a Bank cashier. A pound is worth less than it used to be: in 980 AD, £1 could buy you 15 cows; today it doesn't even stretch to a burger.

SUITS YOU, SIR

Henry Poole decided Savile Row was a good place for his tailor's shop today in 1846, and the world of international menswear would never be the same again. The street soon became *the* place for gentlemen to buy fine clothes. Poole invented the Tuxedo while on Savile Row, originally for the Prince of Wales, but popularised after an American took one home and showed it off at the Tuxedo Club in upstate New York. The word 'bespoke' came from cloth that was said to 'be spoken for' by one of Poole's clients. And the Japanese word for suit is 'sebiro', a corruption of Savile Row.

WATER GOOD IDEA

Before today in 1859, drinking water was so filthy and expensive that London's men, women and children drank beer pretty much all day long. Tough, huh? But then philanthropist Samuel Gurney erected London's first drinking fountain on the corner of Giltspur Street and Holborn Viaduct (it's still there), offering clean water to all. Soon 7,000 people a day were using it and 800 more were quickly built by the Metropolitan Drinking Fountain and Cattle Trough Association. This was the first body of its kind in the world and it's still going today, putting fountains in schools and developing countries.

APRIL

I AM SAILING

Putney-born yachtsman Sir Robin Knox-Johnston sailed into Falmouth today in 1969 and became the first person to make a solo non-stop circumnavigation of the world. He'd spent 10 months alone at sea in his 32ft- (9.8m) boat *Suhaili*. There were seven other sailors attempting the feat as part of a challenge laid down by *The Sunday Times*, but one by one they all dropped out, leaving Knox-Johnston the only finisher. Wouldn't have fancied doing his laundry after a trip like that ...

TO BE PUBLISHED OR NOT TO BE PUBLISHED

World literature and the English language would be much the poorer if it wasn't for two London actors buried in the churchyard of St Mary Aldermanbury. John Heminge and Henry Condell were friends of William Shakespeare and, when the bard died today in 1616, they collected Shakespeare's 36 plays, half of which had never been seen before, and published them as the priceless 'First Folio'. *Macbeth*, *Julius Caesar*, *The Tempest* and many other incredible plays would have been lost forever had these two not collected them.

A PRESENTER WORTH LOOKING UP TO

The first ever episode of The Sky at Night was broadcast by the BBC today in 1957. Presented by Pinner-born stargazer supreme Patrick Moore, the show continued with Moore at the helm until 7 January 2013. This run of 55 years made it the longest-running programme with the same presenter in world television history. The most famous astronomers (on this planet, anyway) have all appeared on the show, as well as astronauts Buzz Aldrin and Neil Armstrong, and Brian May, the guitarist from Queen and an astrophysicist by education.

PICTURE YOURSELF AS A FAMOUS ARTIST

J.M.W. Turner, Thomas Gainsborough and David Hockney – the Royal Academy's Summer Exhibition in Piccadilly has shown off the work of some of England's greatest artists, since it first opened on this day in 1769. But the truly wonderful thing is that the exhibition is open to everyone: if you've done a nice picture of your cat using poster paints, you are welcome to enter it. Just pay your £25 fee and send it in. Go on, you could be the next Constable …

THE MARK OF BRITISH QUALITY

The designer of Tower Bridge, Sir John Wolfe Barry, gathered the country's leading civil engineers together today in 1901. The goal of this 'Engineering Standards Committee' was to standardise steel sizes. They succeeded, cutting the number of tramway rail gauges from 75 to 5 and saving millions. The committee later became the British Standards Institution and their famous Kitemark® became a stamp of quality recognised worldwide.

MOB RULE

It was once a magnificent royal residence, then a fire gutted the Palace of Westminster in 1512. Parliament took over the site, but in 1834 an even greater fire destroyed the buildings. So a national competition was held for new Houses of Parliament, and Charles Barry's design won. Today in 1840, the foundation stone was laid for this magnificent gothic building, which symbolises this country's power, history and heritage more than any other. It was built with one side flush to the river so that an angry mob couldn't surround the building.

CHERRY POPPED OFF

The children of Mr and Mrs J. Lewis Barnes, of Cambridge Square, used to love walking their Maltese Terrier, 'Cherry', in nearby Hyde Park. Kids and dog made particular friends with the gatekeeper, Mr Winbridge at Victoria Lodge, and when Cherry died today in 1881, he let them bury the poor pooch in his garden. The idea caught on, and soon the little patch of ground had become the world's first pet cemetery, with 300 deceased pets interred there, including dogs, cats, birds and even a monkey. It had to close in 1903 because it was taking up too much room.

IF-THOU-HADST-NOT-BEEN-INSURED-THOU-WOULDST-BE-PENNILESS

Nicholas Barbon was one of the all-time great Londoners – he was an MP, a fellow of the Royal College of Physicians, and an influential economist who was the first proponent of the free market. After the Great Fire he launched the world's first successful fire insurance company today in 1681. As a property developer, it was Barbon who connected the City and Westminster for the first time – his developments became the Strand and Bloomsbury. He was also remarkable for having one of the greatest names in history: he was christened Nicholas If-Jesus-Christ-Had-Not-Died-For-Thee-Thou-Hadst-Been-Damned Barbon, his father being something of a godly man.

GAS MASTERS

 The world's first public supply of gas was delivered by the London and Westminster Gas Light and Coke Company, of Horseferry Road. Incorporated today in 1812, the firm built the first gas works in the UK and a network of pipes to supply its coal gas to businesses, houses and street lights. By 1819 nearly 290 miles (467km) of pipes had been laid in London, supplying 51,000 burners. The company became so successful it absorbed most of its competitors and was eventually nationalised in 1949. Ultimately it became British Gas, as you may have deduced from their 19th-century customer service.

MAY

THE GREATEST OF EXHIBITIONS

Hyde Park felt like the centre of the world today in 1851, when the Great Exhibition was opened by Queen Victoria. This was to be a magnificent advertisement of Britain's, and her Empire's, industrial and artistic prowess. In its six-month run, six million people – equivalent to a third of the entire population of Britain at the time – visited the exhibition. Its £186,000 (£16,190,000 today) profit was used to found the now-world renowned Victoria and Albert Museum, the Science Museum and the Natural History Museum. A *slightly* more impressive legacy than the Millennium Dome.

GREAT NEWS FOR INVESTORS, BAD NEWS FOR BEAVERS

2 You might think Tesco owns a lot of land, but that's nothing compared with the Hudson's Bay Company. Founded in London today in 1670 by charter from King Charles II, this is the world's oldest chartered trading company. It was given monopoly trading rights for the area drained by rivers flowing into Hudson's Bay. This turned out to be 40 per cent of Canada, over 1.5 million square miles (3.9 million km²). The company was the largest landowner in the world for much of the 17th and 18th centuries, and dominated the world's lucrative fur trade.

DRAMA KING

3 From the sordid streets of Soho, Richard D'Oyly Carte (born today in 1844) rose to become the world's premier theatre impresario. He first worked as a composer and musician, then a talent agent with Matthew Arnold, James McNeill Whistler and Oscar Wilde on his books. To realise his dream of high-quality English comic opera that the whole family could enjoy, he brought together dramatist W.S. Gilbert and composer Arthur Sullivan. He then founded his eponymous theatre company to produce their very successful productions. With his profits he built two theatres and the country's first luxury hotel, the Savoy. The short alley that leads to the hotel, Savoy Court, is the only street in the UK where you must drive on the right.

ROLLS AND ROYCE TAKE OFF

Charles Rolls, an upper-class motoring enthusiast of Berkeley Square, met engineer Henry Royce for the first time today in 1904. They decided to work together towards the simple goal of making the finest motor cars in the world. This they achieved, in considerable style. Their company is still making rides for the rich and famous today, as well as exceptional aircraft engines. Unfortunately, Rolls also went down in history as the first Briton to be killed in a flying accident, in 1910.

REAL-LIFE TV HEROES

These days, with ex-SAS men filling bookshop shelves and eating unmentionables in TV jungles, it's hard to believe that there was a time when no one knew what the regiment was. The SAS was set up as a Special Forces regiment in 1941, but it wasn't until they stormed the terrorist-held Iranian Embassy in London live on TV, today in 1980, that they became famous. Abseiling onto balconies, the SAS used frame charges and stun grenades to blast their way in, killing five of the six militants, rescuing 19 hostages and launching dozens of careers.

ANYTHING DAD CAN DO, I CAN DO BETTER

 After his dad designed St Pancras (see 14 March), architect Giles Gilbert Scott thought he'd better make his mark on London too. So, as well as designing Battersea Power Station and Waterloo Bridge, he created that ultimate British design classic – the red phone box. This was actually the sixth attempt at creating a national phone kiosk, and so was called K6 when it rolled out today in 1935. There were 73,000 in Britain by 1980 and, although many have since been replaced, around 2,000 have listed status.

GOING UNDERGROUND

7 It's the biggest building site in Europe, and the best thing about it is you can hardly see it. Crossrail is the continent's largest construction project, with 10,000 workers on 40 sites. Today in 2012 a pair of crazed mechanical moles – sorry, tunnelling machines – began boring 26 miles (41.8km) of new tunnels with a remarkable degree of finesse. At Tottenham Court Road the tunnel was threaded over the Northern Line and under an escalator with just 3¼ft (1m) clearance on either side. If it continues to go to plan Crossrail will open in 2018.

THE BRILLIANT BARRIER

8 London's position by a tidal river might be scenic, but it does make the city vulnerable to flooding. In 1953 a huge North Sea storm killed thousands and caused millions of pounds worth of damage. A bold idea was needed to protect the capital, and after years of study, discussion and construction, the Thames Barrier was officially opened today in 1984. This engineering marvel is raised when a predicted storm surge combines with unfavourable tides and river flow, holding back floodwaters. Climate change doubters may like to note that the barrier was raised four times in the 1980s, 35 times in the 1990s and 75 times in the 2000s…

THAT'S THE WAY TO DO IT!

With its themes of husband-beating, baby-dropping and crocodile-killing, the traditional Punch & Judy show is British entertainment at its best. The pugilistic puppet show made its debut in Covent Garden today in 1662, as recorded by diarist Samuel Pepys. The figure of Punch came from the Italian trickster character of Pulcinella, and the show was originally very much aimed at adults. By Victorian times it was more child-friendly (if still very violent) and youngsters have been 'pleased as Punch' ever since.

ART FOR ALL

London's National Gallery isn't the world's biggest (that's the State Hermitage museum in Russia) but it is splendid and, importantly, free to enter since it first opened, today in 1824. Originally opened in a townhouse at No. 100 Pall Mall with just 38 paintings, this soon became far too small as the collection grew, and in 1832 construction began on a landmark building in the then-new Trafalgar Square. To this day it is still one of London's top draws for tourists.

BUILT WITH BLADDERS IN MIND

When a statue of the 1966 World Cup-winning captain Bobby Moore was unveiled today in 2007, it marked the opening of the new Wembley stadium. This magnificent arena is the most capacious in Britain and one of the largest in the world, with room for 90,000 sport-mad spectators. And don't worry if you overdo the pre-match refreshment, Wembley also boasts the most lavatories of any venue on the planet – 2,618 to be exact.

A NEW POWER IN THE ART WORLD

It's the number one modern art gallery in the world – Tate Modern, with 4.7 million visitors per year. Rather than knock down the derelict Bankside Power Station, in 1992 the Tate Gallery had the brilliantly simply idea of turning the old building into a thing of beauty itself. The gallery opened on this day in 2000 and more than 40 million people have visited since then. The spectacular five-storey-high Turbine Hall lets visitors walk in and around the art, to wonder what the hell it's meant to be from every possible angle.

WHO SAID CRIME DOESN'T PAY?

Today in 1787, 11 ships crammed with convicts left to establish a penal colony in Australia – the first European settlement Down Under. Shipping your convicts off to the other side of the world was a simply brilliant idea. You no longer had to feed and clothe them and they couldn't escape and start nicking things again. It's even more awesome for the convicts: 'Let me get this straight – you want me to leave this dingy, rat-infested, filth-strewn cell in the basement of Newgate prison and go to … Botany Bay? Er, okay.' No wonder there was so much crime in Victorian England – they were all gagging to be transported.

BRYAN'S CAN-DO ATTITUDE

How to feed the soldiers of a distant and growing British Empire was a thorny problem. For 300 years, seamen had been eating salted meat and hardtack biscuit, and malnutrition killed thousands. Then south London merchant Bryan Donkin perfected the tin can as a means of food preservation. He opened the world's first canning factory and supplied the Navy today in 1813 with tins of beef, mutton, carrots, parsnips and soup. Mind you, no one invented the can opener until 1855, so for decades a hammer and chisel, a bayonet or a rock had to do the job.

IT HURTS EITHER WAY

The Puckle gun, patented today in 1718 by ingenious London inventor James Puckle, was the world's first machine gun. That's not a very nice thing to boast about, but the invention itself was at least eccentric in a very English way: it could fire round bullets at 'civilised' enemies and square bullets at Turks. Puckle reasoned that since the square shot caused more damage, this would convince the Turks of the benefits of our Christian 'civilisation'.

THE LADY WITH THE LAMP

Florence Nightingale rebelled against her upper-class family to become a nurse, famously tending to the injured soldiers in the Crimean War. She was caring *and* effective, reducing the army hospital death rate from 42 per cent to 2 per cent by making improvements in hygiene. Her book *Notes on Nursing* was the first of its kind and a classic guide to the profession, and the nursing school she started at St Thomas' Hospital in London was the first secular nursing school in the world. Its first graduates began their lives of care today in 1865. The Nightingale Pledge taken by new nurses was named in her honour, and every year International Nurses Day is celebrated worldwide on her birthday.

SAVING DAYLIGHT
TO WASTE IT IN STYLE

Ah, those long summer evenings, when you get home and there's still time to grab a beer and relax in the sun! Well, you can thank William Willett from Chislehurst for them. He was out riding early this morning in 1907 when he noticed how many blinds were still down, and he had the bright idea for daylight saving time. He proposed advancing clocks at the start of summer to save electricity and gain evening light. When World War I brought an urgent need to save coal, Britain introduced the scheme, and many other countries soon copied the clock-changing, beer-enjoying idea.

ARE YOU A FAN FAN?

If so, then you need to get to Greenwich's Fan Museum, the only museum in the world dedicated entirely to fans. (The wafting-air-at-you type, not the really-liking-something-a-lot sort.) Opened today in 1991, it has more than 4,000 fans from around the world, from the 11th century to the present day. Fashionable fans, practical fans, historical fans, ceremonial fans – there are splendid examples of them all. In fact, of London's 240 museums, this is easily the coolest.

COMIC STRIP

19 It wasn't the most promising of starts, when the Comedy Store opened in a depressing space above a strip club in Soho today in 1979. But the club become an institution where every young comedian came along to get heckled. French & Saunders, Alexei Sayle, Craig Ferguson, Rik Mayall, Adrian Edmondson, Ben Elton, Simon Pegg, Paul Merton and Mike Myers all got their first big laughs on its tiny stage. It's still the city's busiest comedy venue and the most influential comedy club on the planet. No kidding.

SHINY HAPPY PEOPLE

The first Pearly King was Henry Croft, a Victorian ratcatcher. London's costermongers (street fruit sellers) then wore suits decorated with pearl buttons on the seams. Henry went one step further and completely covered a suit in pearls, including top hat and tails. He became famous and used his celebrity to raise money for charity. His colourful look and voluntary work were embraced by those embodiments of happy cockneydom, the Pearly Kings and Queens. Today they hold their annual Memorial Service in Trafalgar Square.

ANTIQUE ANTICS

21 Mooching about Portobello Road market is one of the great London traditions – particularly for the hordes of tourists who insist on doing just that every weekend. Still, this is the largest weekly antiques market in the world, gathering 1,000 dealers of all sorts of collectibles from gorgeous old clocks to terrifying ceramic cats. The market was famously immortalised in the film *Notting Hill*, which premiered today in 1999. This was about a down-to-earth local bloke falling in love with a movie star – well, a down-to-earth local bloke who looked like Hugh Grant, that is.

THEY KEPT CALM AND CARRIED ON

When the last palls of smoke cleared today in 1941, the Blitz was over. For the last eight months, one week and two days London had been bombarded by the Luftwaffe 71 times. More than one million houses were damaged and 20,000 people killed. The bombing was intended to demoralise us into surrender and damage the war economy – but it did neither. Londoners just got on with things, like going to the pub and the cricket at Lord's, while casually comparing raids to the weather, saying that a day was 'very blitzy'. After all, if you can handle rush hour at Waterloo, you can handle anything.

VAST AND AMAZING

Even if you went every day and viewed 100 objects every visit, it would take you 126 years to see all 4.6 million treasures in the Victoria and Albert Museum. By which time they'd probably have added a few million more. It's the world's largest arts and design museum, and it was founded today in 1852. Its 145 galleries cover 12½ acres (5ha), taking visitors through 5,000 years of artistic creation. No wonder it became the first museum in the world to have refreshment rooms.

IT LIVES ...

The blood-curdling tale of the monster created from spare body parts and galvanised into life is one of the most haunting and influential stories of all time. Incredibly, *Frankenstein* was written by an 18-year-old London girl, Mary Shelley. She spent the wet summer of 1816 with the poets Percy Shelley and Lord Byron, each writing stories for the others' amusement. Mary completed her tale today in 1817 and originally the monster didn't have a name – Victor Frankenstein was his creator.

A QUALITY ESTABLISHMENT, I'LL WARRANT

A Royal Warrant above a shop door is a sure sign of high quality (and perhaps of high prices, now that we think about it). King Henry II of England gave the first Royal Charter to London's Weavers' Company in 1155, and the practice flourished, particularly in Victorian times. Today in 1840 the Royal Tradesmen's Association was formed to help promote the 'best of the best', and there are now around 850 Royal Warrant holders, ranging from Aston Martin to Tom Smith's Christmas crackers.

A VOYAGE OF DISCOVERY

Almost nothing was known about the ocean depths until Woolwich-built HMS *Challenger* returned home today in 1876. She had been converted into a floating laboratory for a four-year voyage of 68,890 nautical miles (127,666km). Scientists on board had discovered more than 4,700 new species and laid the groundwork for the entire discipline of oceanography. They first sounded the deepest part of the world's oceans, paying out 4,475 fathoms (26,850ft/8,184m) of line before touching bottom in what's now called the Challenger Deep. The US space shuttle *Challenger* was named after her.

CHELSEA'S BLOOMING MARVELLOUS

 Officially it is known as the Great Spring Show, but to most garden fans it is simply the Chelsea Flower Show, the most famous horticultural event in the world. First held today in 1862, it gives gardeners the chance to catch the latest plant trends in what is a virtual catwalk for the gardening world. It is also simply very beautiful, and every year 157,000 visitors come to check out the tulips.

SHARP-THINKING STANLEY

 If you ever used a pair of compasses to draw a circle at school (or even to stab your mate in the leg) then you've benefited from William Ford Stanley's genius. Islington-born Stanley was the world's foremost maker of precision drawing and surveying instruments, who used his fortune to found the UK's first Trades School, Stanley Technical Trades School, and to build the Stanley Halls in South Norwood. He also held 79 patents for inventions as diverse as rotary engines, cameras, electric batteries, a height-measuring machine (patented today in 1889) and, most importantly, an improved lemon squeezer.

HAVE YOU GOT YOUR TRAVEL MONEY?

29 It started off in Regent Street as a boozy dining club for toffs who liked going places, but the Royal Geographical Society has perhaps done more than any other body to further our understanding of our world. It was founded in 1830 by scientists including Sir Francis Beaufort (of wind speed scale fame) and has since supported dozens of famous expeditions, including those of Charles Darwin, David Livingstone, Henry Stanley, Captain Robert Scott and Sir Ernest Shackleton. Today in 1953, Sir Edmund Hillary and Tenzing Norgay stood atop Mount Everest, thanks to the Society's cash.

CHARITY SHOP CHAMPIONS

30 Whether you're a Christian or not, every Londoner can get behind the Salvation Army – they certainly do a mean carol service. The Army was founded by Methodist minister William Booth and his wife Catherine today in 1865, as the East London Christian Mission, which offered soup, soap and salvation to the city's down-and-outs. Since its first international conference in London today in 1886, it has become one of the world's largest providers of social aid, blowing its trumpet in 126 countries.

HEATHROW TAKES OFF

Usually it's somewhere you curse rather than feel proud of, but Heathrow Airport (which opened today in 1946) really is exceptional. It's the world's busiest international airport, and the busiest overall in Europe. It's incredible how much has changed here in one human lifetime: in 1929, Terminal 1 was 'Heathrow Farm' with miles of orchards and market gardens all around. Now 90 airlines use the airport to fly 69 million passengers to 170 destinations worldwide, with a plane landing or taking off every 45 seconds.

JUNE

POLAR ROVER

It's hard enough finding the North Magnetic Pole nowadays – the pesky thing moves 35 miles (56.3km) a year. Back in 1831 it took a very intrepid gentleman from London by the name of James Clark Ross to pin it down on this day as it meandered across the wastes of northern Canada. Ross was a truly great explorer whose name is attached to a rather large area of the world: the Ross Sea in Antarctica is named after him, as is the Ross Ice Shelf and Ross Island. He also discovered Mount Erebus and Mount Terror, two Antarctic volcanoes.

THERE'S NO GLASS CEILING IN THIS GAME

2 Elizabeth Alexandra Mary is the full name of a London girl who today in 1953 got herself one heck of a promotion. At the age of just 25, young Liz suddenly became Queen Elizabeth II, monarch of England, the United Kingdom, Supreme Governor of the Church of England, queen of 16 independent sovereign states, the figurehead of the 54-member Commonwealth of Nations and later the patron of over 600 charities and other organisations. How she finds the time to walk her corgis I don't know. Gawd bless her!

HE COPIED HIS BEST IDEA

3 David Gestetner was born in Hungary, but it was in north London that he made his mark on our civilisation. In the 19th century business was handicapped by the need to painstakingly copy contracts and letters by hand, often 50 copies at a time. Then Gestetner patented (today in 1881) the stencil method of duplication using wax paper. Suddenly dozens of copies could be made in minutes, boosting business – and free speech. Now people could cheaply print and distribute, uncensored, ideas that printers wouldn't dare touch.

LONDON CALLING

When Guglielmo Marconi took his early work on radio transmission to the Italian government, the minister he met recommended the young inventor be sent to the lunatic asylum. Perhaps taking this too literally, Marconi promptly set off for London. Here he gained the support of fellow crazy scientist William Preece, who persuaded the Post Office to pay for most of Marconi's major breakthroughs. The world first saw (or heard) the amazing new transmission medium at the Royal Institution today in 1897.

MAKING PENTONVILLE LOOK PALATIAL

London has had more prisons than any other city in the world – there were 18 by the 17th century, as well as 60 whipping posts, stocks and cages. There were specialist jails for criminals, religious dissenters, careless politicians and debtors – thousands were jailed for the equivalent of not paying off your credit card, including Charles Dickens' father. Southwark's notorious medieval prison, the Clink, was the oldest in England and gave its name to prisons in general. It was burned down by rioters today in 1780 and thankfully never rebuilt.

THERE'S NO NEED TO FEEL DOWN

A cowboy, a construction worker, a biker, a police officer, a soldier and a native American got together in London today in 1844 to found one of the world's great social aid institutions ... Actually, the YMCA was founded by a draper called George Williams. He was shocked by the terrible living conditions of youths working in London so he created a safe, Christian place for them to stay, far from the temptations of alcohol, gambling, prostitution and handlebar moustaches. Today the YMCA has 125 national associations and helps more than 58 million people every year.

DEDICATED FORERUNNER OF FASHION

Why do we wear suits and ties? Ask Beau Brummell, the famous dandy of Regency England – it was his idea. Born in London, today in 1778, Beau claimed it took him five hours to dress and that he polished his boots with champagne. He established the gentlemen's fashion of tailored dark suits with full-length trousers worn with a cravat, and this good-looking combination evolved into the staple business-wear the world over. Way to go, Beau.

SIGN OF THE TIMES

You might think those 'golf sale' board guys have stamina, but they're a bunch of lousy amateurs. The world's most-dedicated human billboard was Stanley Green from Harringay. From this day in 1968 he stood and walked on Oxford Street carrying his large homemade sign six days a week for 25 years. His board bore the wise legend: 'Less Lust, By Less Protein: Meat Fish Bird; Egg Cheese; Peas Beans; Nuts. And Sitting.' He sold a pamphlet of his teachings for 7p; on the cover it noted: 'this booklet would benefit more, if it were read occasionally.'

THE ART OF CARTOGRAPHY

Before all this new-fangled GPS technology, we relied on Ordnance Survey maps to get us lost in the middle of Dartmoor, which they've been doing since this day in 1791. The government, wary of invasion from revolutionary France, instructed the Board of Ordnance to accurately survey the south coast of England. Having successfully done this by 1801, the OS went on to map the whole of Britain, which took more than 20 years. It was the first national topographic survey in the world and it started with a 5-mile (8km) baseline surveyed on Hounslow Heath, now part of Heathrow Airport.

TRENTON STICKS HIS OAR IN

10 The Boat Race is one of the most famous sporting events in the world, with millions watching every year on TV and around 250,000 lining the riverbank. The very first one took place on this day in 1829 at Henley-on-Thames, before later moving to Putney. It's a notoriously tough race, being held no matter how nasty the conditions. Cambridge sank in 1859 and 1978, Oxford in 1925 and 1951, and both boats went down in 1912. The main difficulty in 2012 was protestor Trenton Oldfield, who decided it was a good idea to jump into the chilly, murky Thames and buzz the boats.

THE CRYSTAL AMAZES

11 Imagine if Charlie Dimmock had designed the Millennium Dome – that's roughly what happened with the Crystal Palace. The Great Exhibition of 1851 was to be a showcase for Britain's industrial and artistic brilliance, and it needed an exhibition hall. Today in 1850, Joseph Paxton, a celebrity gardener of his day, drew up plans for the largest glass building the world had ever seen. Covering 19 acres (7.6ha) of Hyde Park, the structure was 1,851ft (564m) long and 128ft (39m) tall – so vast it included many of the park's trees, along with their sparrows. These made such a mess that a sparrowhawk was employed to scoff them all.

RISEN FROM THE ASHES

London's original Globe theatre, beloved of Shakespeare, was destroyed by fire in 1613. But 384 years later, a fabulous replica opened on the South Bank, today in 1997. A performance of *Henry V* gave the audience as realistic a taste of Elizabethan theatre as the modern world can offer. The Globe itself is as close to the original circular playhouse as possible: made of English oak, it has a thrust stage, three tiers of steep seating, space for 700 'groundlings' and the first and only thatched roof permitted in London since the Great Fire of 1666.

PRINCE OF POETS

One of the greatest of all our poets and the first to be buried in Westminster Abbey, Geoffrey Chaucer got his first commission today in 1374, for *The Book of the Duchess*. But it was his epic *Canterbury Tales* that would truly shape English – and indeed world – literature. This was totally radical for its day with its vivid naturalism, variety of stories and the spiciness of the characters. Chaucer was the first English poet to use the five-stress line, a cousin to the iambic pentameter, and he helped standardise the London dialect of Middle English. He also ensured there were plenty of rude bits to keep future schoolkids awake.

THE ROCK BEGINS TO ROLL

The first tourists began queuing in the rain outside a Hard Rock Café today in 1971 when the very first such restaurant opened its doors in Piccadilly. The memorabilia-clad walls only started in 1979 when Eric Clapton asked the manager to reserve his favourite table by hanging his red Fender guitar above it. Pete Townshend did the same, and within a few years the café chain was the largest rock 'n' roll collector in the world. It has an archive of 70,000 items in 175 Hard Rock locations across 53 countries.

NEWS JUST IN – MILLET TO DOUBLE IN PRICE

When Paul Julius Reuter established his news agency at the London Royal Exchange today in 1851, he still transmitted many of his stories by carrier pigeon. But he soon moved onto telegraphy and developed his business into the world's largest news agency. The agency later moved to Fleet Street, where its headquarters became something of a training ground for brilliant thriller writers – Frederick Forsyth and Ian Fleming both first bashed a typewriter there.

BATTERIES NOT EVEN NEEDED

When ex-stuntman Trevor Baylis saw the plight of AIDS victims in Africa on telly, he promptly hurried off to his garage on Eel Pie Island and invented the wind-up radio. Patented today in 1993, his ingenious device needs no batteries, just a few seconds' winding and then it's all ready for eager listeners to receive broadcasts of news, music, or even Chris Moyles.

BROOM-BROOM-BROOKLANDS

The leaders of Britain's motor manufacturers attended a luncheon near Weybridge, today in 1907, to inaugurate the world's first purpose-built motorsport venue – Brooklands. Many world records were set on its banked oval in the next 20 years, including the 24-hour distance record. Brooklands became one of Britain's first airfields, with an aerobatic display in 1909 in front of 20,000 spectators. A Vickers aircraft factory was built here, and after World War II motor racing ceased. However, it once again entered the record books in 2009, when the *Top Gear* team built the world's longest Scalextric track round the remains of its circuit – 2¾ miles (4.4km) long.

NOT ON YOUR LIFE

A London salter named William Gibbons took out the world's first life insurance policy today in 1583. This is particularly notable because, even then, the underwriters tried to wriggle out of paying. The term was 12 months and Gibbons duly expired within that period on 29 May 1584. But his heirs were astonished to hear the underwriters claim that 'month' meant a period of 28 days, and so the policy had expired. It went all the way to court before Mr Gibbons was favoured.

PEELERS HIT THE STREETS

Before this day in 1829, law and order in London was maintained by volunteer constables and watchmen. And there wasn't that much of either. As the Industrial Revolution drove exponential growth of the capital, this part-time force became ineffective at crime-fighting. Home Secretary Sir Robert Peel recommended a new style of police force: an official, paid profession, organised in a civilian rather than military way. Crucially, it should also be answerable to the public. And so the world's first modern police force was born.

LONG TO REIGN OVER US

When Kensington-born Queen Victoria succeeded to the throne today in 1837 it was one of the most significant moments in English history. Just 18 when crowned, she became a national icon, reigning for 63 years and seven months, longer than any other British monarch and the longest reign of any female monarch in history. The Victorian Era saw a flourishing of British industry, culture and science, as well as the expansion of the British Empire, which eventually covered around a quarter of the planet.

THE WEIGHT OF THE WORLD

You see some strange and wonderful things on Clapham Common (especially after dark), but perhaps the most remarkable was the 'Cavendish Experiment' (published today in 1798). Scientist Henry Cavendish built an ingenious experimental apparatus in his Clapham laboratory that used a torsion balance and large lead balls to measure gravity. Incredibly sensitive for its time, his experiment generated values for the gravitational constant (G), our planet's mass and its density – to within 1 per cent of the modern figure. Cavendish also discovered hydrogen in 1766.

TWO HUNDRED (YEARS) NOT OUT

Lord's (named after its founder, Thomas Lord) is the spiritual home of world cricket. The ground hosted its first match today in 1814, between Marylebone Cricket Club and Hertfordshire. Lord's also has the world's oldest sporting museum, which contains hundreds of years of celebrated cricket memorabilia, including the Ashes urn (the one the players hold up is a replica). The actual pitch is also remarkable because it has a significant slope: the northwest side of the ground is 8ft (2.4m) higher than the southeast side.

LONDON'S SILVER MINE

Deep under Chancery Lane is one of London's oddest shopping streets – the London Silver Vaults. The 30 shops in this underground alley offer the world's largest collection of silver for sale. The vaults opened in 1876 as a safe deposit service and are certainly secure: the building above was obliterated by a German bomb in the war, but the vaults were undamaged. They reopened in 1953 as a series of secure underground silver shops and are claimed to be so heavily fortified that theft has never even been attempted. Which is surely tempting fate.

WHO KEEPS ATLANTIS OFF THE MAPS?

They designed the pyramids, launched the French Revolution and are keeping the flame burning for the Knights Templar – so the conspiracy nuts say about the Freemasons, the ultimate secret society. Who knows what they're really up to, but what is certain is that the United Grand Lodge of England on Great Queen Street was founded today in 1717 and is the oldest Grand Lodge of Freemasons in the world. It's the hub for six million Freemasons, a brotherhood that's the world's oldest and largest non-political and non-religious organisation. And the oddest, frankly.

THE COST OF FREE SPEECH

Many parts of the world have a Speakers' Corner, where orators can stand up and speak their mind on pretty much any subject (if they don't mind a bit of humorous heckling). The tradition was born today in 1855 when 200,000 irate citizens demonstrated here, in the northeast corner of Hyde Park, against a bill banning any form of trading on Sundays – the only day the working classes had off. Twelve years later, protests here forced the government to grant working men the vote. Karl Marx, Vladimir Lenin, Marcus Garvey, William Morris and George Orwell have all ranted here, at a spot that for 600 years was the site of the Tyburn gallows.

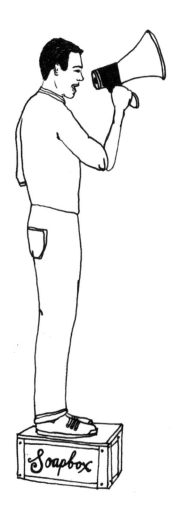

DNA DAY

Scientists from the Sanger Centre in London handed over the decoded human genome to the world today in 2000. They had unravelled 85 per cent of the three billion DNA base pairs – the blueprint for every aspect of your body, from the capillaries in your lungs to the colour of your eyes. Effectively all the ingredients that makes you *you*. The Human Genome Project could benefit every human on Earth and many believe it is modern science's greatest achievement.

ANOTHER TENNER MACHINE

Given that our banks are open for about four hours a day, it makes sense that we invented the cash machine. The world's first proper ATM was installed at Barclays Bank in Enfield Town today in 1967 and first used four days later by actor Reg Varney. Today there are 1.7 million worldwide. The pioneering Enfield machine was also the first in the world to be vandalised. One in eight men admit to using a cash machine but being too drunk to remember it. Which would explain why nights out seem to cost so much.

I COMPUTE THEREFORE I AM

Some people are so far ahead of their time it's scary. Charles Babbage was born in London back in 1791, but he had the foresight to invent the first practical computer – the Difference Engine. This mechanical number-cruncher would have been 11ft (3.3m) long, had 8,000 moving parts and weighed 5 tons – if only Victorian engineers had been able to follow his advanced designs. It wasn't until the Science Museum built a replica and turned it on today in 1991 that they discovered it worked perfectly. It could even print its results!

PLASTIC NOT FANTASTIC

From the toys in our Happy Meals to the carrier bags in our trees, we surely couldn't think of a life without plastic. One of the world's greatest inventions, the first true plastic was invented by metallurgist Alexander Parkes. He brought his Parkesine (based on cellulose nitrate) to world attention at the Great International Exhibition in London today in 1862. Despite winning a prize medal and establishing his own company, he was not successful, partly because 'Parkesine' had a tendency to burst into flames.

GETTING A RISE AT TOWER BRIDGE

Tower Bridge was the largest bascule bridge in the world when it opened today in 1894. It is now one of the most famous of all London landmarks. Its massive 1,000-ton bascules are still raised (in just five minutes) around three times a day. For a long time it was also the world's most recognisable pick-up joint. The high-level walkways had to be closed in 1910 because they were being used almost exclusively by swarms of prostitutes and their punters.

JULY

OUT AND ABOUT

 Europe's largest gay and lesbian population helps make London perhaps the world's most cosmopolitan city. The first official UK Gay Pride Rally was held here today in 1972, with around 2,000 participants. Now hundreds of thousands of LGBT revellers and their friends celebrate Pride Festival every summer. While Soho's main drag of Old Compton St is London's year-round hotspot for gay cruising and occasional outrageousness.

WATER COPPERS COME A CROPPER

2 The Thames River Police is the world's oldest organised police force (as opposed to the constables of a single borough), first brandishing their waterproof truncheons today in 1798. They were really more of an 18th-century version of G4S, being set up to combat the pilfering going on around London's docks. This wasn't easy – at first there were 50 constables policing 33,000 river workers, 11,000 of whom were known criminals. Still, they saved £122,000 worth of cargo (and a few lives) in their first year, later inspiring Robert Peel's 'bobbies'.

KEEN'S CREAM OF THE CROP

It's the perfect London summer experience – tucking into strawberries and cream at Wimbledon and happily paying a fortune for the privilege. But strawberries were once only available a few weeks a year, being notoriously hard to grow. Then an Isleworth market gardener called Michael Keens spent years developing new varieties of strawberries. Today in 1806 he exhibited the first successful large-fruit cultivar from which all our modern strawberries are descended. It's thanks to him that Wimbledon can sell 61,730lb (28,000kg) of the fruits during the tournament, doused with 12,320 pints (7,000 litres) of cream.

(NOT) RINGING THE CHANGES

Whitechapel Bell Foundry is Britain's oldest manufacturing company. It has made bells, more bells and nothing but bells since 1570, when Queen Elizabeth I was on the throne, and may have been in business as far back as 1420. Its famous bells include Big Ben (at 13½ tons their biggest casting), the Great Bell of Montreal and the Liberty Bell, which Americans celebrate as a symbol of their independence today.

I'LL BET THIS TAKES OFF

It was a normal 18th-century Friday evening in the City of London until a man appeared, running from Cornhill to Cheapside, out of breath and utterly naked. He was duly arrested and when asked by the bewildered constables why he was doing what he was doing, the chap cheerfully admitted it was for a wager of 10 guineas (worth £735 today). And so the modern sensation of streaking was born. In its birthday suit, obviously.

ART IN THE HEART OF THE CITY

Every city has its great statues, but only London has the Fourth Plinth. Built in 1841, the plinth in Trafalgar Square was meant to carry an equestrian statue of William IV, but the money ran out. It stood empty for 150 years until Mark Wallinger's *Ecce Homo* statue of Jesus was unveiled today in 1999. The idea of putting a modern sculpture up there was a sensational hit, and since then the plinth has been a unique venue for temporary artworks.

LYCRA-CLAD LEGEND

It was a big day for British cycling fans today in 2012 – Kilburn's own Bradley 'Wiggo' Wiggins took the yellow jersey in the Tour de France. He didn't relinquish it for the next 15 days, crossing the finish line in Paris to become the first-ever English winner of the prestigious cycle race. Countryman Mark Cavendish won the final stage, and Chris Froome was second overall. Froome went on to win it himself the following year. Wiggo, of course, took gold the following month in the London Olympics.

TOP OF THE DOCKS

8 If docks knock your socks off, then get ready to go barefoot – London's Royal Docks were the largest in the world when the third and final in the complex, the King George V Dock, opened today in 1921.

With its neighbours the Royal Albert Dock and the Royal Victoria Dock, they had 250 acres (101ha) of water and an estate of 1,100 acres (445ha) – the same as the whole of central London from Hyde Park to Tower Bridge. Their 12 miles (19.3km) of quaysides could berth hundreds of cargo and passenger ships at once. Closed in 1980, they are now home to London's City Airport, which lies between Albert and George and makes passengers think they're going for a swim on every landing.

THE ORIGINAL MAJOR TOURNAMENT

9 The Championships, Wimbledon, is the oldest tennis tournament in the world and the most prestigious. It has been held at the All England Club in the London suburb of Wimbledon since this day in 1877 and is the only major championship still played on grass.

And quite right too. When Walter Clopton Wingfield, a major in the 66th (Berkshire) Regiment of Foot, invented the game during a party on his estate in 1873, it was on his garden lawn.

THE BBC IN SPACE

Telstar, the first satellite to supply a live transatlantic television feed, and the first privately sponsored space launch, was blasted into orbit today in 1962. Although launched by NASA, it was actually co-designed by the General Post Office and internationally co-ordinated from the BBC Television Centre in London. It also successfully relayed through space the first telephone calls and fax images.

THE SINGING STATION

Waterloo Station (opened today in 1848) is one of the world's biggest and busiest stations, with 88 million passengers a year passing through its barriers. That's over 240,000 travellers a day (in case you don't have a calculator to hand). Until 2009, the station even had its own police station, with three cells. Its name derives from the scene of a famous military victory, Wellington's final defeat of Napoleon in 1815. It's also the scene of one of the most melancholically English of pop songs, 'Waterloo Sunset', by The Kinks.

CRIMINALLY PROFITABLE

The Moonstone, by Wilkie Collins, was published today in 1868 and almost single-handedly launched one of the most popular of all fiction genres: the detective novel. Collins' tale includes several elements that would become staples of this type of story, including a robbery in a country house, a skilled investigator, bungling local plods, red herrings, a 'locked room' murder, a reconstruction of the crime, and a twist in the tale. It also sold absolute bucketloads, spawning many an imitator.

WHO'S WHOM

Readers of the *St James's Chronicle* in 1780 would this morning have seen this advertisement: 'John Debrett begs leave most respectfully to acquaint the Nobility and Gentry and his readers in general that he is removed from the late Mr William Davis's the corner of Sackville Street to Mr Almon's Bookseller and Stationer, opposite Burlington House, where he hopes he shall be honoured with their commands.' The ad obviously worked: this is the same Debrett whose name has for more than two centuries adorned *the* reference tome of the English nobility. And if you need to check – no, you aren't in it.

ED'S ON TOP OF THE WORLD

14 Teddington isn't the most obvious of proving grounds for mountaineers, but it was the home of Edward Whymper, the most accomplished British mountaineer who nobody has heard of. He became the first person to climb the Matterhorn, a peak that had long been thought of as impregnable, today in 1865. It was his ninth attempt. Whymper made many other first ascents in the Alps, the Rockies, and bagged the first ascent of Chimborazo, the highest mountain in Ecuador – and the world, if you measure from the centre of the Earth to its summit.

'DO YOU LIKE KIPLING?'

15 'I don't know, you naughty boy, I've never kippled!' so runs the joke on the world's best-ever selling postcard, a six-million seller by Donald McGill from Blackheath. In a 59-year career this king of saucy postcards produced 12,000 designs that sold 200 million copies. He rated his own cards mild, medium or strong in vulgarity; 'strong' were the best sellers. George Orwell was a big fan, but the authorities weren't: McGill was famously tried and found guilty of obscenity, today in 1954. He was almost 80.

THE SERVICE THAT'S NOT SECRET ANY MORE

No one admitted that one of our country's greatest institutions existed, despite everyone knowing full well that it did, until today in 1993. For that's when the Secret Service decided to blow its own cover. Stella Rimington became MI5's first Director General to pose for the cameras in London as she launched a brochure outlining the organisation's activities. When MI5 later began advertising job vacancies, it received 12,000 applications from wannabe Bonds on the first day alone.

CARTOON CAPERS

It's thanks to *Punch* that today we refer to a humorous illustration as a 'cartoon'. The famous magazine first appeared in London today in 1841 and was hugely influential for most of its life until it faded out in the 1990s. Its gentle, sophisticated English wit was enjoyed by readers from Charlotte Brontë to Queen Victoria, it could boast Charles Dickens as an editor and on its drawing staff were E.H. Shepard (who illustrated *Winnie-the-Pooh*) and John Tenniel (who illustrated *Alice's Adventures in Wonderland*).

PUBLISHING IS CHILD'S PLAY

Children's publishing was revolutionised today in 1744, when John Newbery had the radical idea of printing something that children might want to actually read. *A Little Pretty Pocket-Book* had rhymes, jokes, pictures and a free gift, and flew off the shelves. It also had the first recorded mention of 'Base-Ball'. Newbery went on to publish over 100 more from his premises in St Paul's Churchyard. He had authors of the calibre of Samuel Johnson and Oliver Goldsmith, who wrote Newbery's most popular book, *The History of Little Goody Two-Shoes*.

BRUNEL BRIDGES THE WORLD

When it comes to engineering excellence, there is one Londoner who stands in particular esteem: Isambard Kingdom Brunel. He built famous bridges (including the Clifton Suspension Bridge), dockyards and the Great Western Railway, for which he designed the viaducts, tunnels, stations and even the locomotives. He constructed the world's first tunnel under a river (the Thames Tunnel) and his *Great Britain* was the first steamship driven by a screw propeller, while the *Great Western* (launched today in 1837) was the largest and fastest ship in the world and made the transatlantic voyage in record time.

THE BEST PLAICE IN TOWN FOR FISH

The Romans unloaded all sorts of cargoes at Billingsgate, but it was made a specialist fish market by a very exact act of Parliament in 1699 (lobsters could be no less than 8in [20cm] long). It became the biggest fish market in the world when its grand new home, designed by Sir Horace Jones, opened today in 1877. Although it has now moved to the Isle of Dogs, it is still the largest in the UK. And the smelliest.

A BIRD IN HAND

Today you can see the very bizarre tradition of 'Swan Upping' on the River Thames heading to its triumphant finale. Five days ago, men from the Dyers' and Vintners' Companies of the City of London piled into rowing boats and set off from Sunbury on a 70-mile (112.7km) voyage to Abingdon. On the way, they surrounded all the swans they saw, caught them, counted them and then released them. You might wonder what the point of this is – after all, it's not like the elegant creatures are endangered or even in scarce numbers. Well, we've been doing it since the 12th century, it's a tradition and that's all there is to it.

PLIMSOLL PROVOKES PARLIAMENT

We can sympathise – Samuel Plimsoll bellowed in rage at the Prime Minister today in 1875. And he had the bottle to unleash his fury in Parliament itself. Plimsoll's Merchant Shipping Act aimed to stop overloaded ships putting to sea but it was being scuttled by ship-owning MPs. Vested interests, the honourable members? Surely not! Anyway, his outburst worked, and the Act was passed. It established, among other safety measures, the mark indicating a ship's loading limit, now known worldwide as the Plimsoll line. This new law helped save thousands of sailors' lives.

THE SPEED KING IS CROWNED

Today in 1955, English speed king Donald Campbell set his first world record when he shot across Ullswater in his jet-boat *Bluebird K7* at a tourist-terrifying 202.15mph (325kph). The Surrey-born speedster would go on to break more water speed records than anyone else, and to become the only person to break the land and water speed records in the same year (1964). Tragically, Campbell died when *Bluebird* crashed during another record attempt in 1967.

OTTERLY BRILLIANT

Where is Europe's largest wetland creation project – Norfolk? Yorkshire? Scotland? Try Walthamstow. A hugely ambitious scheme to transform ten Thames Water reservoirs into Europe's biggest urban wetland nature reserve got the go-ahead today in 2014. The reserve will be colossal – at 494 acres (200ha) it's bigger than Richmond Park and Hampstead Heath. The 300,000 local residents, many of whom are water voles, are said to be delighted.

A VERY WELLCOME DONATION

A sad day this, in 1936, for pharmaceutical magnate Sir Henry Wellcome – he died. But the good news was that his enormous legacy was used to set up the Wellcome Trust in London, now one of the largest charities in the world. It has £16.6 billion in its coffers, which it spends on scientific research and training to improve human and animal health. Sir Henry's unrivalled personal collection of medical curiosities is on display at Euston Road – it includes Napoleon's toothbrush.

WE WILL NOW MAKE THIS WINE DISAPPEAR

London is officially the most magical city on Earth – if measured by number of professional magicians. That's because it's the worldwide home of the Magic Circle, the trade guild of illusionists and tricksters. It was founded today in 1905 by 23 top magicians on a boozy night out at London's Pinoli's Restaurant. It was going to be called the 'Martin Chapender Club', but that wasn't very mysterious, so Magic Circle it was. It has 1,500 members (including, bizarrely, Prince Charles), and all are sworn to secrecy about where they keep their rabbits.

THE OLD LADY RULES THE WAVES

1690 – England had been trounced at sea by France and was broke. The Government was so untrusted it couldn't get credit (ha!). Then the Earl of Halifax set up something very special in Walbrook: a new corporation to take on the government's balances, inject some cash, and issue bank notes backed by bonds that could be traded. £1.2m was raised in 12 days, half was spent on a spanking new navy, industry leapt into top gear and soon Britannia ruled the waves. The corporation moved to Threadneedle Street in 1734 and is better known as the Bank of England.

YOU SAY 'LEE-DO', I SAY 'LY-DO'

More than just a south London institution, Tooting Bec Lido is the UK's largest swimming pool at 100 yards (91m) long and 33 yards (30m) wide, and holds 1 million gallons (4.5 million litres) of water. It's also officially one of the country's coldest – sorry, *oldest* – open-air pools. The public first dipped their tootsies in its crystal waters today in 1906, when women were only allowed in one morning a week. Then, however, it was called the Tooting Bathing-Lake – it wasn't referred to as a 'lido' until 1935.

A ONCE IN A LIFETIME OPPORTUNITY (NO, REALLY)

Today you can watch the return of the comet named after one of the world's greatest astronomers, Edmond Halley from Haggerston – if you're reading this in the year 2061, that is. He was the first man to work out that comets return regularly: the comet seen in 1682 was the same one that had appeared in 1607 and 1531. Halley's Comet is one of the nippiest things in the solar system, clocking 157,838mph (254,009kph). Halley also stumped up the cash for the publication of Newton's *Principia Mathematica*, one of the most important scientific documents of all time.

WHAT WOULD THE
NUNS MAKE OF IT NOW?

Many of the most elegant town squares in the world's great cities owe their existence to this day, when architect Inigo Jones began building a church and three terraces of fine houses around the walled garden of an old convent west of the City. The open, elegant design of Jones's new square had a stunning impact, setting the template for many more squares as London grew, and influencing town planning worldwide. Covent Garden (with spelling mistake) became a fruit and vegetable market that survived until the 1960s and is now one of the world's busiest shopping and entertainment areas. Fittingly enough for an old fruit market, the largest Apple Store in the world opened in the Piazza in 2010.

PLATFORM 6
FOR THE INSANITY EXPRESS

 The St Bethlehem Royal Hospital was founded at Bishopsgate in 1247, and was the world's first hospital dedicated to mental illness. Historically, care was somewhat less enlightened than today – whips and chains were the standard 'treatment' and visitors paid to see the lunatics as an entertainment. Its shortened name – Bedlam – became synonymous with uproar. It moved to a leafier, more soothing Kent location today in 1930. The hospital's original site is now Liverpool Street Station, which, in its own way, continues the seven-century tradition of mayhem.

AUGUST

ROW, ROW, ROW YOUR BOAT
RAPIDLY UP THE STREAM

Doggett's Coat and Badge is the oldest rowing race in the world, pre-dating that other boat race by over a century. It was first organised today in 1715 by an Irish actor, Thomas Doggett, who offered the prize of a red jacket, a badge and considerable renown for the waterman who could row from London Bridge to Chelsea the fastest. At 4 miles 5 furlongs (7.5km) in length, it's the Grand National of rowing races, although thankfully they don't make horses compete.

CAPITAL CONFUSION

Thank goodness for Henry I. This third Norman King of England might be obscure, but if it wasn't for him the history of our great city – and country – could be very different. When Alfred the Great was crowned King of Wessex in 871 AD he established Winchester as his capital. The first two Norman kings, William I and II, kept Winchester as their capital because it was only 14 miles (22.5km) from Southampton, where they could catch a ship to their homeland of Normandy. Henry I (crowned today in 1100) had the good sense to make London the nation's capital city – after all, Winchester doesn't even have an IKEA.

NEASDEN'S ANSWER TO THE TAJ MAHAL

Turn off Brentfield Road in Neasden and you might feel you've suddenly been transported 4,000 miles (6,437km) to India. For there in front of you is Swaminarayan Mandir, Europe's first traditional Hindu stone temple and the largest Hindu temple outside India. This modern wonder began life today in 1992 when the first of 2,828 tons of limestone and 2,000 tons of marble, carved by a team of 1,526 Indian sculptors, arrived on site. It opened for worship three years later. Its restaurant does a famously good veggie curry, and holds the world record for most vegetarian dishes served – 1,247.

BOWLED OVER

Two London hatmakers, Thomas and William Bowler, got an unusual order today in 1849. A toff called William Coke wanted a strong, close-fitting hat lower than a top hat to protect the heads of his family's gamekeepers. When he collected his hat he placed it on the floor and stamped hard on it twice; the hat withstood this test and Coke paid 12 shillings for his 'Bowler'. Today it's one of the most popular images of Englishness. But the bowler, not the cowboy hat or sombrero, was the most popular hat in the American West.

WHERE MILLIONAIRES ARE TEN-A-PENNY

It's official – when it comes to money-grubbing monomaniacs grabbing all the cake, we are world-beaters. Figures released today in 2014 show that London is the millionaire capital of the world, beating those peasants in Tokyo, New York and Hong Kong. One in every 35 London residents – 376,600 people – have more than $1m to their name. Of course the fact that they're making all that cash by charging us extortionate rent is neither here nor there.

WWW.LONDONERSARETECHYGENIUSES.COM

For work, shopping, socialising and timewasting on a biblical scale there has never been anything like the World Wide Web. And it was created by Londoner Tim Berners-Lee, who was working at CERN in Switzerland when he needed a way of managing the vast amount of information held at the research laboratory. So he built the first web server, browser and site, and put them online today in 1991. Approximately 90 seconds later a woman in Ruislip posted a picture of her cat with a box on its head.

AUGUST

THE MELTING POT METROPOLIS

You can hear an incredible 300 languages spoken in London, and that's just by minicab drivers. There are 50 non-indigenous communities with a population of more than 10,000. Which is particularly wonderful if you like trying unusual restaurants. No wonder it was proclaimed today in 2012 as the most culturally diverse city in the world. How do we know for sure? Well, David Cameron announced this impressive fact, and if anyone knows about diversity, it's him, right?

PLAY TIME

When you see the new *Time Out* cover on the newsstands, you know your London weekend is here. The very first magazine was published today in 1968 as a 16-page pamphlet listing happening events, as well as Blueish Films, Puppets and Rabbit Food. People loved the city-focused idea and there are now 46 editions in 30 countries. *Time Out* was once pretty radical – in 1976 it published the names of 60 CIA undercover agents in England. Nowadays it's 60 secret burger stands – but hey, that's still fun.

LIVE IN LONDON

9 An Austrian violinist named Leopold realised that his two musically gifted children could earn more than him if they toured the European courts. And so Wolfgang Amadeus Mozart (and his sister Maria) came to live in London for a year of some of his most formative experiences. The Mozarts performed three times at Buckingham House (now Buckingham Palace) for King George III and Queen Charlotte. Their skint father also had them busking in pubs to raise much-needed cash. And today in 1764 Mozart completed his very first symphony, while living at No. 180 Ebury Street, in Belgravia. He was eight years old.

PROMS FOR THE PEOPLE

10 When impresario Robert Newman organised the first Promenade concert in London today in 1895, he wanted to attract people from all walks of life, particularly those who might not normally appreciate classical music. His proms had low prices and an informal atmosphere in which eating, drinking and smoking were encouraged. His tradition continues today: the prom season has over 100 concerts in auditoriums and parks across the country, as well as educational and children's events.

BLYTON BANNED

From the moment her first slim book of poems *Child Whispers* sold out its print run in 1922, Enid Blyton from East Dulwich (born today in 1897) was destined to be a publishing phenomenon. She often wrote as many as 50 books a year, and kids devoured her tales of the Famous Five, Secret Seven and Noddy. However, many schools, libraries and the BBC banned her books for 'lacking literary merit'. Still, as she sold more than 600 million books in 90 languages, the BBC can stick their merit up their Malory Towers.

THREE-TIME WINNER

A unique Olympic hat-trick was notched up by London today in 2012 – it was the third time we had hosted the Summer Olympics. No other city has done so. (We hosted in 1908 and 1948, too.) It was also an awesome home performance athletically – our stars of track and field won 65 medals, 29 of them golds. Add to that the sensational opening ceremony, amazing stadia and all-round feel-good factor, and London 2012 has to go down as the best £9 billion ever spent.

THE MASTER
OF...SUSPENSE

Born the son of a Covent Garden greengrocer (today in 1899), Alfred Hitchcock became the most influential filmmaker of all time. He started out designing the titles for silent movies at Gainsborough Studios, before moving into the director's chair from where he helmed more than 50 feature films over six decades, including the classics *Psycho*, *The 39 Steps* and *North by Northwest*. He also coined the term 'MacGuffin' for the extremely-important-but-totally-arbitrary object pursued by everyone in a movie, without which most thrillers would have no plot.

SIZE IS NO LONGER IMPORTANT

London might not be the world's biggest city any more, but it is the most influential. That's according to analysts at *Forbes*, who put us ahead of New York, Paris and Singapore in a report today in 2014. The City's unparalleled reputation as a global financial capital was a key measure, as were London's marks in eight other categories including foreign investment, technology and media power. Add this all up, subtract a bit for the weather and – boom, we're still number one.

AUGUST

YOU WON'T BELIEVE WHERE
HE JUST PUT HIS HAND

A man walked onto a stage with a wooden doll on his arm tonight in 1886, and light entertainment changed forever. Fred Russell from Poplar was a journalist who became a world-famous pioneer of ventriloquism. Then, all other ventriloquists talked to a group or family of figures. Fred was the first to use a single dummy ('Coster Joe') and to have it sitting on his knee. He established the classic act of quick-fire verbal interplay in which the 'vent' is the 'straight man' and the dummy cracks the jokes. Fred was incredibly popular for decades, and he did more than any other performer to shape the art of ventriloquism. Apart from his dummy, of course.

THE RAGGED SCHOOL PHILANTHROPIST

Great swarms of poor, sick and homeless children once roamed the darker, dirtier streets of Victorian London. Then in 1844, the Ragged Schools Union was founded to give free education, food, clothing and lodging to these urchins. It revolutionised how society treated the destitute, with 300,000 children attending London ragged schools between 1844 and 1881. One man, Dr Thomas Barnardo, opened 112 such schools under his own name. Today in 1990, the Ragged School Museum opened in the largest of his old schools to celebrate their life-changing charity.

LET'S DRINK TO OUR LOOPY LAWS

In London it is illegal to carry a plank along a pavement, enter the Houses of Parliament wearing a suit of armour and beat a carpet in the street (you can beat a doormat, but only before 8am). Nor can you fly kites, play annoying games (does Candy Crush count?), or slide on ice or snow in the street. And, since today in 1839, it's also an offence to be drunk on licensed premises. I'd like to see them police that one.

COP SHOP SWAPPED FOR MOP PROP

In the southeast corner of Trafalgar Square is a cylindrical stone booth with a tiny door that is actually the world's smallest police station. Measuring 3ft (0.9m) across and made from a hollowed out lamp-post, it had an internal light, a telephone line connected to Scotland Yard and a large lantern on top, supposedly from Nelson's flagship *Victory*. The station first opened for duty today in 1926. Now it's used as a broom cupboard for street cleaners but, alas, is not the world's smallest one of those.

READY, STEADY ... COE!

One of the greatest purple patches in all of world athletics was enjoyed by Hammersmith-born Sebastian Coe today in 1979. In July he had already bagged the 800m and mile world records and today he became the fastest man ever to run the 1500m – that made three major world records in 41 days. He is also the only person ever to win successive Olympic 1500m titles.

THE EVOLUTION OF MODERN SCIENCE

A dusty, book-lined room in the Linnean Society in Burlington House on Piccadilly is where the world first heard the most radical and far-reaching idea in all science. A paper by Charles Darwin and Alfred Wallace on evolution 'by means of natural selection' was presented here and then printed today in 1858. Darwin published *On the Origin of Species* the next year, a book that triggered a paradigm shift in biology and has become one of the most influential ever written.

THE NOBLEST OF NIBBLES

In the wee hours of this night in 1762, the 4th Earl of Sandwich was ensconced at the gaming table of the Shakespeare's Head pub in Covent Garden. Too busy to bother with a formal dinner, he demanded of the waiter: 'Just bring me a piece of meat between two bits of bread.' His chums thought the snack looked dandy and said: 'Bring us what Sandwich is having.' And so the world got its favourite multi-decker lunchtime delicacy. Someone probably *had* eaten such a thing before, but they weren't an earl and so no one paid any attention.

WHAT TIME DOES THE MUSEUM OPEN?

Switzerland is now famous for its watches, but for centuries it was London, particularly Clerkenwell, that was the world centre of clockmaking. The Worshipful Company of Clockmakers was founded today in 1631 and is the oldest surviving horological institution in the world. Its museum is also the oldest, and has the finest collections of clocks, watches and sundials on the planet. In 1796, an incredible 191,678 gold and silver watches passed through Goldsmiths' Hall to be stamped.

THE BRIDGE
THAT WAS AHEAD OF THE REST

For 500 years London Bridge was one of the architectural wonders of the world. Completed in 1209, it was 900ft (274m) long and its 19 arches supported 200 buildings, many up to seven storeys high and overhanging the river by 7ft (2.1m). The roadway on this extraordinary street was a frantic burrow just 12ft (3.7m) wide, which took an hour to traverse. The bridge also had the world's finest display of severed heads. The first – William Wallace's – was spiked there today in 1305 and there were always 30 or so on display.

THE CARNIVAL COMES TO TOWN

24 It's the largest street celebration in Europe – the Notting Hill Carnival. Every year up to two million revellers throng the Portobello streets to party and pee in people's doorways. And it all started today in 1964, when a mere 100 merrymakers enjoyed the inaugural event. A group of Trinidadian immigrants decided to throw an impromptu procession through their neighbourhood, complete with steel band. The spectacle caught the English public eye and Carnival was here to stay.

BECAUSE THERE'S NO HONOUR IN DEFEAT

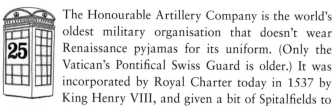

25 The Honourable Artillery Company is the world's oldest military organisation that doesn't wear Renaissance pyjamas for its uniform. (Only the Vatican's Pontifical Swiss Guard is older.) It was incorporated by Royal Charter today in 1537 by King Henry VIII, and given a bit of Spitalfields to practice archery on. Today it lives on as a Territorial Army unit. The HAC's longevity may be explained by its flexible approach to loyalty: it fought on both sides during the English Civil War.

THE BEAT GOES ON

Medical science took another huge leap forward today in 1994 when doctors fitted the world's first battery-operated heart into 62-year-old London man Arthur Cornhill. Poor Arthur had been given only months to live – then he got the chance to be a history-making guinea pig. Tony Stark does this kind of thing to himself, but in the real world it took an 11-person team of the world's leading heart surgeons to plug in the new titanium and plastic pump. Although, fittingly for such a bold operation, Mr Cornhill was a retired movie stuntman.

FEELING A BIT LIVERY THIS MORNING

The 100 livery companies of the City of London have a proud history as medieval trade guilds, but now mostly do a power of good raising money for charity. (And raising the glasses of their members.) Today in 2005 the Mercers announced they had donated £9 million to charity in the last year alone. The livery companies have a strict hierarchy based on founding dates – the Company of Mercers is the oldest, Arts Scholars is the newest. However, the Merchant Taylors and the Skinners can't agree who was founded sixth and seventh, so they swap precedence every Easter. Hence the phrase 'at sixes and sevens'.

AM I NOT A MAN AND A BROTHER?

William Wilberforce led a group of worshippers in the Holy Trinity Church, Clapham Common, who gave themselves a community challenge just a wee bit harder than organising a fête – abolishing slavery. At least 11 million Africans were enslaved by Britain, with 1.4 million dying in the process. William decided to end this brutal trade in 1787 and for the next 46 years he fought a parliamentary battle that culminated in triumph with the Slavery Abolition Act today in 1833. This abolished slavery throughout the British Empire, and Wilberforce's anti-slavery movement became a prototype for later humanitarian campaigns.

SOUTHWARK'S SMARTEST SON

Michael Faraday was a humble blacksmith's son from Newington Butts who happened to be a scientific genius. Today in 1831 he discovered electromagnetic induction – how a change in magnetic intensity can produce an electric current. Soon after he discovered that electricity was generated when a magnet passed through a helix wound with wire. He thus invented the transformer and dynamo, key elements of the electric motor. It was largely thanks to Faraday that electricity could be put to practical use. He is easily one of the most influential scientists in history.

MOUNT UNPLEASANT

30 The Post Office opened Mount Pleasant Sorting Office in Clerkenwell today in 1889, and for decades it was by far the largest in the world. It even had its own underground railway, known as Mail Rail, running for 6½ miles (10.5km) from Paddington to Whitechapel. It was one of the first sorting offices to use optical character recognition when it introduced a machine in 1979. The office was originally built inside a dingy old prison, and the name was an unsubtle attempt to shake off the jail's reputation for making its inmates do tedious manual labour in gloomy surroundings. Current employees are divided on whether this worked.

BIG, BOLD, BEAUTIFUL BARBICAN

31 Londoners often overlook the Barbican – which is tricky as its apartment towers are 123 metres tall – but this London landmark really is worthy of our pride. Springing from an overgrown, rubble-strewn bombsite, the estate buildings were topped out today in 1976 as the tallest residential towers in the city. And the Barbican Centre is the largest performing arts centre in Europe. It was built by the City of London Corporation and opened by Queen Elizabeth II in 1982. The Council then presented the Barbican as a gift to the nation – thanks!

SEPTEMBER

KICKING THE HABIT

1 It seems obvious now, but before this day in 1950, people had no concrete evidence that smoking was linked to lung cancer and heart disease. In fact, tobacco companies often highlighted their products' health *benefits*. Then physiologist Richard Doll (with Austin Hill) studied lung cancer patients in 20 London hospitals and discovered that smoking was the only factor they had in common. Doll stopped smoking himself and today published his findings in the *British Medical Journal*.

THAT'S ONE WAY TO
SPRING CLEAN THE PLACE

The Great Fire of London, which started today in 1666, was tragic for the city's inhabitants but it was probably a good thing for England in the long run. London had been a filthy, overcrowded warren of a capital; the fire incinerated many slums and all traces of the previous year's plague, and the devastation allowed the capital to be rebuilt in brick and stone, not wood. The new streets were wider and cleaner and many beautiful new public buildings were created, including St Paul's Cathedral.

THE CLUTTER THAT SAVED HUMANITY

Don't you hate it when you get back from holiday and your desk is in a mess? Biologist Alexander Fleming certainly did when he returned to his laboratory in St Mary's Hospital, London, today in 1928 – there were contaminated bacteria cultures all over his workbench. Luckily though, while he was away, a fungus had killed patches of bacteria. Fleming was amazed, and he soon developed that fungus into penicillin, the most efficacious life-saving drug in the world. It would conquer syphilis, gangrene and tuberculosis among many other infections, saving an estimated 200 million lives to date.

THE MOD SQUAD

With their sharp suits, Italian scooters and distinctive hairstyles and music tastes, Mods were a major part of British youth culture in the '50s, '60s and '70s. 'Mods' came from 'modernists', reflecting the group's origins among young fans of 'modern' jazz. The term encompassed a whole subculture, but the movement was first brought to a wider audience in London writer Colin MacInnes's cult novel *Absolute Beginners*, which was published today in 1959.

THE 1ST CLASS BOOKSHOP

Next time you pick up a Brontë or Dickens novel at the station, you can feel proud that your purchase is possible thanks to William Henry Smith from London. He introduced the world's first railway bookstall, at Euston in 1848. Which would have sold Brontë and Dickens. It proved rather popular, and the company became the world's first chain store, WH Smith. Smiths has managed many other innovations, including creating the ISBN book catalogue system in 1966. And William Smith Jnr was the first person to publish (today in 1856) the claim that Francis Bacon was the author of Shakespeare's plays.

BRUNEL'S BIG BABY

There's big, and then there's gi-bloody-normous. When the SS *Great Eastern* sailed out of a Millwall shipyard on her maiden voyage today in 1859, she was six times larger by volume than any vessel afloat. Designed by engineering legend Isambard Kingdom Brunel, she was 692ft (211m) long with a tonnage of 18,915 – so vast she had to be launched sideways into the river. She could carry 4,000 passengers from England to Australia without refuelling. After retiring as a liner, *Great Eastern* laid the first lasting transatlantic telegraph cable in 1866. She is still the largest sailing ship ever constructed.

THEY WERE DEAD GOOD

If there's one thing that London's excellent at, it's killing brilliant young rock stars. The city's streets are sadly haunted by more than its fair share of musically talented ghosts: Amy Winehouse, Marc Bolan, Jimi Hendrix, Bon Scott and Freddie Mercury. Mama Cass and Keith Moon (who died today in 1978) even managed to meet their maker in the very same flat in Shepherd Market, Mayfair. There must be something in the water (or the drugs).

BROAD STREET IS A SNOW-GO AREA

In 1854 cholera outbreaks killed thousands in London and Dr John Snow went to the streets of Soho to investigate. By carefully mapping the cases he discovered that a water pump in Broad Street was the centre of the outbreak. A cesspit had contaminated the well. Today he begged authorities to intervene by the simple action of removing the pump's handle; they were sceptical, but did so. The outbreak faded away. Snow's work was one of the biggest events in the history of public health and helped to found the science of epidemiology.

THE FLYING POSTIE

London notched up another pioneering achievement on this day, when the world's first scheduled airmail postal service took off. It may only have linked the suburb of Hendon with Windsor in Berkshire but, then again, it was not bad for 1911. So dramatic was the event that King George V even gave permission for the aeroplanes to land in the grounds of Windsor Castle. However, of the four planes meant to fly the service, only one made it – the other fragile bi-planes were grounded due to high wind.

THE CARAVAN MAN

10 Londoner Yannick Read made history today in 2014 when he set the Guinness World Record for building the world's smallest caravan. The tiny leisure vehicle, which is fully roadworthy, is just 7ft 11in (2.4m) long, 5ft (1.5m) high and 2ft 8in (0.8m) wide. Which is still bigger than the average Tufnell Park flat. Yannick's next project is a flying bicycle, which will travel at 15mph (24.1kph) on land and 25mph (40.2kph) in the air, and need no licence to use. London's cabbies will be delighted to see that on the streets.

THE MAN WITH THE MIDAS TOUCH

11 One man who shaped the London skyline more than most was architect Ernő Goldfinger (born today in 1902). His Brutalist tower blocks, such as Trellick Tower in North Kensington, were loathed but many are now listed buildings. When author Ian Fleming heard how notoriously bad-tempered Goldfinger was, he named his baddie after him. Ernő threatened to sue; Fleming threatened to change his villain's name to Goldprick. The architect backed off. Incidentally, Fleming named another baddie after cricket commentator Henry Blofeld's dad, whom he didn't get on with at school.

WHAT'S THE POINT OF ITS NAME?

It may be one of London's best-loved monuments, but Cleopatra's Needle is also surely the least accurately named. Erected on the Thames Embankment today in 1878, the 68ft (20.7m), 224-ton red granite obelisk was gifted to us by Egypt to commemorate victories at the Battle of the Nile in 1798 and the Battle of Alexandria in 1801. But the obelisk is almost 3,500 years old, meaning it was already extremely ancient by the time Queen Cleopatra VII came to the throne in 51 BC.

LIKE BLUEWATER, BUT FOR DICTATORS

When our Forces were hunting for those elusive WMDs in Iraq, they should have popped down to Docklands and saved everyone a bit of bother. For today in 2013 saw the climax of the Defence and Security Equipment International (DSEI) event at the ExCeL centre – better known as the world's largest arms fair. Record numbers of guns, missiles, tanks and other killing devices were sold by 1,500 firms to 30,000 delegates including representatives from such democratic strongholds as Turkmenistan, Uzbekistan and Bahrain. Quick, Uzis are on 2-for-1!

HANDEL'S HIGHLIGHT

Today in 1741, George Frideric Handel finished his *Messiah*, a monumental musical masterpiece. Living in London and by then a naturalised citizen of these shores, Handel wrote the work in English. It is one of the world's most popular oratorios and its 'Hallelujah' chorus is a particular Christmas favourite. The two-hour piece had taken him just 24 days of inspired composing to create.

HARRY WAS FRAMED

When thief Harry Jackson stole a set of billiard balls from a house in Denmark Hill, he could hardly have thought that he would go down in history. But Jackson made the mistake of stealing the balls from a house that had just been painted, so leaving a fingerprint on a window frame, just as Scotland Yard was perfecting its fingerprint detection procedures. Harry became the first person in the world to be convicted from fingerprint evidence, and today in 1902 he started seven years in prison. Crime fighters – and crime writers – had a handy new weapon.

HEROIC HUDSON FADES FROM HISTORY

Henry Hudson was one of the greatest, and most unsung, of all explorers and he was a Londoner. Today in 1609 he sailed up the river in New York that now bears his name. Hudson County, the Henry Hudson Bridge, the Hudson Strait, and the town of Hudson, New York are also named after him. So too is the huge bay, twice the size of the Baltic Sea, that he discovered the following year. His obscurity is possibly because he actually thought Hudson Bay was the Pacific Ocean and his crew got so hacked off that they cast him and his son adrift, never to be seen again.

THE NAME'S MARTIN, ASTON MARTIN

Lionel Martin loved racing cars at Aston Hill and when he met engineer Robert Bamford they decided to start their own high-quality car company. They took premises at Henniker Mews in Kensington where, in March 1915, they produced the very Aston Martin. The company almost went under several times, until the classic 'DB' series sealed its reputation in the 1950s and '60s. And when James Bond ejected a baddie from a silver DB5 in *Goldfinger* (which premiered today in 1964), that marque became the most famous in the world.

OPENING FIGHT

18 When the Covent Garden Theatre reopened tonight in 1809 after burning down the previous year, the management put their ticket prices up from six shillings to seven. The London theatre-going public duly rioted for the next 65 days straight. And quite right too. Today the West End is the world's premier theatre destination, with 14,587,276 tickets sold in 2013. And with the average ticket price now £46, surely it's only a matter of time before we kick the hell out of Covent Garden. Well, we would if 14,587,000 of those tickets hadn't been sold to rich tourists…

THE ORIGINAL COMPUTER GEEK

19 Clive Sinclair from Richmond founded his revolutionary electronics company today in 1973, and within a few short years he put Britain at the forefront of home computing. His ZX80, brought out in 1980, had a tiny 1 KB of memory (it would take a million of them to match today's average laptop), but cost just £99.95, bringing it within reach of the average household for the first time. Two years later, Sinclair launched the ZX Spectrum; kids persuaded their parents they needed one for school, it became Britain's bestselling computer and a whole generation of brilliant boffins was born.

DUELLING DIPLOMATS

Londoners are honourable people, and in the 18th century this trait made the city the duelling capital of the world. Duelling was illegal, but was the decent, if deadly, way to settle a dispute. Dozens were fought every year and there was even a list of 26 insults that no gentlemen should allow to pass. Hampstead Heath, Chalk Farm and the windmill at Wimbledon were favourite duelling grounds. Prime Ministers William Pitt and the Duke of Wellington fought duels. Lord Castlereagh even challenged his fellow cabinet minister, Foreign Secretary George Canning, today in 1809. Canning missed and Castlereagh shot him in the thigh. Come on, Osborne and Clegg – pistols at dawn!

WORLD-BEATING BEATS

It seems hard to believe that when DJ James Berkmann had the idea of making the sound system the most important thing in a club, rather than the décor, it was revolutionary – but it was. Revellers first shook their things in his Ministry of Sound tonight in 1991, and this disused bus garage in Elephant & Castle soon became the ultimate club for dance-music purists. It now attracts 300,000 clubbers a year, has hosted sets from every superstar DJ who's ever spun a disc, and won 'World's Best Sound System' four years in a row.

THE RELUCTANT TENANTS

10 Downing Street may be one of the most famous addresses in the world, but it has to be the least impressive abode for a nation's leader. Today in 1735 the first Prime Minister to live there, Sir Robert Walpole, moved in. But the house proved shoddily built, and has had to be reconstructed several times. During the last renovation, builders found its facing bricks were actually yellow, but had been darkened by centuries of soot – so they painted them black to save the bother of cleaning them. Prime Ministers generally detest living there, and frankly, we like it that way. Stops them getting ideas above their station.

LEND HER A BLUNDERBUSS

When news of Bonnie Prince Charlie's victory over Government forces at the Battle of Prestonpans reached London today in 1745, the leader of the band at the Theatre Royal, Drury Lane felt such a frenzy of patriotism that he had 'God Save The King' performed after a play. This was a terrific success and the custom of greeting monarchs with the song as he or she entered a place of public entertainment was formed. Curiously, there is no authorised version of the National Anthem – it's a matter of tradition. So there's no reason why you can't change the words a little if you fancy it.

KITCHEN KILLERS

There was a time when foreigners laughed at the state of our capital's grub. And it was pretty minging, to be fair. But now you can be proud that you live in one of the planet's gourmet hotspots. There are 6,128 licensed restaurants in London – that's 22 per cent of the tally in the whole of Britain, a higher ratio than for any other international capital. You can dine on menus from more than 50 overseas cuisines, from Iceland to Ethiopia. And, as of today in 2014, there are 63 eateries with Michelin stars. Just don't mention the Angus Steakhouses.

BEATING THE YANKS IN THEIR OWN BACKYARD

The world land speed was smashed today in 1997 by Wing Commander Andy Green, who clocked an incredible 714.144mph (1,149.3kph) in Nevada's Black Rock Desert in his jet-powered car, ThrustSSC. He later raised this record to 763.035mph (1,227.9kph), becoming the first man to break the sound barrier on land. This was just the start for a new project dreamed up in the London's Department for Innovation, Universities and Skills and announced at the Science Museum. Green is planning to break the 1,000mph (1,600kph) mark in the rocket-powered car Bloodhound SSC. This will smash the record by 33 per cent – the highest margin ever.

HAIR WE GO

The country welcomed the dawn of a new era of cultural freedom with the abolition of theatre censorship today in 1968. The new Theatres Act ended the Lord Chamberlain's powers of censorship, which dated back to 1737. The very next day the hippy musical *Hair*, which featured nudity and drug-taking, opened in London. The countercultural revolution of the late 1960s had broken down another barrier, never to be put up again.

THE COUNTING COUNTESS

Who wrote the world's first computer program and when? No, it wasn't a geeky guy with glasses in the 1950s, but Countess Ada Lovelace, the daughter of Lord Byron, today in 1843. The London-born Countess was a mathematician who befriended Charles Babbage, designer of the Difference Engine, a prototype mechanical computer. Ada wrote an algorithm for him, the very first designed to be run on a machine, making her the most glamorous, aristocratic and unlikely of boffins.

STUFFED WITH TALENT

University College London may be several centuries younger than Oxford and Cambridge, but it has a pretty impressive history nonetheless. William Ramsay discovered the noble gases neon, argon, krypton and xenon here, and 28 alumni have won Nobel Prizes. It was the first university to admit students regardless of their religion, and to admit women on equal terms with men (today in 1878). It's also the last resting place of brilliant philosopher and reformer Jeremy Bentham, whose body was preserved and put on public display in a wooden cabinet, as per his wishes.

FIRST, CATCH YOUR HARE

Forget Nigella and Delia, the original domestic goddess was 23-year-old London housewife Mrs Isabella Beeton. Her recipes began appearing in *The Englishwoman's Domestic Magazine* today in 1859, and were a sensation. Beeton's innovations included a list of ingredients at the start of recipes and illustrations so you could see how badly you'd gone wrong. Two years later they were collected as her famous *Book of Household Management*, which became the authority on all things domestic and culinary, even if it did recommend boiling carrots for two hours.

OO, YES PLEASE, TWO SUGARS

'That Excellent, and by all Physicians approved, China drink, called by the Chinese, Tcha, by other nations Tay alias Tee, ... sold at the Sultaness-head, ye Cophee-house in Sweetings-Rents, by the Royal Exchange, London.' So ran the ad in the magazine *Mercurius Politicus* today in 1658. It had been placed by Thomas Garraway, a coffeehouse owner in London, and marked the European debut of our number one drink, tea. In the coming centuries the product was nurtured by the Empire and London became the world centre of the tea trade.

OCTOBER

THE SWEET TASTE OF SUCCESS

Silvertown might not be the most attractive part of the Thames (okay, it's an industrial armpit), but it is home to a world-leading business. The humungous Tate & Lyle refinery supplies 40 per cent of Europe's entire sugar cane. Lyle's Golden Syrup has been produced there since 1885, and today in 2006 it was officially named Britain's oldest brand. It also qualifies as our weirdest brand, with its logo of a dead and rotting lion being infested by bees showing today's advertising creatives what edgy really is.

GLOODY GRILLIANT NEW INVENTION

The very first image seen on TV (today in 1925) set the tone for the vast majority of subsequent programming: it was the head of a ventriloquist's dummy. Television's Scottish inventor, John Logie Baird, did his breakthrough work in Soho, where he built the world's first working television using a tea chest, a hatbox, a pair of scissors, some darning needles, some bicycle light lenses, sealing wax and glue. He later invented colour TV and gave the first public demonstration of TV in Selfridges department store on Oxford Street.

THIS IS STILL THE AGE OF THE TRAIN

It's difficult to imagine when you've been stuck outside Stevenage for two hours, but the InterCity 125 train is actually one of our country's great successes. The first one left Paddington for Bristol Temple Meads today in 1976 and, amazingly, arrived three minutes early. The world's fastest diesel train still covers 1,000 miles (1,600km) a day, seven days a week. Its unique shape is thanks to designer Kenneth Grange from London, who created two other design icons: the Kenwood Chef and the parking meter.

HOPPING THE POND

Boeing and Airbus rule the world of aircraft manufacture now, but London was a pioneer in the jet airliner industry – the first ever transatlantic jet passenger service was launched today in 1958 by Heathrow-based BOAC. Passengers could hop between New York and London on the new de Havilland Comet in the record time of six hours and twelve minutes.

WAKLEY HEALS THE WORLD

The Lancet has been at the cutting edge of medical knowledge (literally – a lancet is a double-edged scalpel) for nearly two centuries. It was first published in London today in 1823 by Thomas Wakley, an English surgeon and firebrand reformer. Wakley hated 'quackery' and as well as establishing the world's first peer-reviewed medical journal, he became a radical MP who campaigned fearlessly against incompetence, privilege and nepotism.

THE LONGEST TAIL IN THE THEATRE

6 *The Mousetrap* has now reached the point where the very fact that it is an English institution will draw the tourists and so ensure its continued survival, regardless of any inherent quality. Agatha Christie's murder mystery with a shocking twist ending was first performed today in 1952. It has now clocked up more than 25,000 performances and is still running at the St Martin's Theatre, giving it the longest initial run of any play in history. Christie, not anticipating its success, gave the rights of the play to her grandson as a birthday present.

THE BOMB IS BORN

7 Hungarian theoretical physicist Leó Szilárd was working in exile in London in 1933. On this cool autumn morning he was standing on the corner of Southampton Row and Russell Square, waiting for the cars to pass and pondering a recent speech by famous physicist Ernest Rutherford that dismissed atomic energy. The lights changed, Szilárd stepped into the road and was immediately hit by a revelation (he was lucky, it could have been a 59 bus). His London traffic-inspired brainwave was that an element could be made to undergo a nuclear chain reaction. Thus the Atomic Age was born in the leafy streets of Bloomsbury.

THERE'S NO TOWER HERE, GUV

When the Post Office Tower opened today in 1965 it was the tallest building in the country. But because its main purpose was to carry telecommunications traffic, some of which might be sensitive, the tower was officially a secret, and did not appear on Ordnance Survey maps until the 1990s. Despite it being 581ft (177m) tall and built in central London.

SUMOS SIZE UP

The first sumo wrestling tournament ever staged outside Japan waddled into action in the Royal Albert Hall today in 1991. A sell-out crowd of 5,000 watched the men-mountains do battle in the sacred dohyo of South Kensington. It was the first contest on foreign soil in the sport's 1,500-year history, making this a terrific honour for London. And a bumper day for the local Pizza Hut.

WORLD'S FIRST WEATHER OBSESSIVES

10 The summer of 1848 was so wet and horrible (some things never change) that there were serious fears for Britain's harvest. To assuage the public, or to scare them into buying more papers, the editors of the *Daily News* commissioned Mr J. Glaisher, Superintendent at the Royal Observatory and Britain's first full-time meteorologist, to create the world's first daily weather report. Glaisher got his daily information from 29 railway stationmasters (27 in England, two in Scotland) via telegraph. Today's report in that year was 'generally wet'. At least there were no leaves on the line.

THAT'S A BLOODY GOOD IDEA, PERCY

11 An emergency at King's College Hospital today in 1921 resulted in a frantic call to the Camberwell branch of the Red Cross for a blood donor. This new medical procedure so impressed the Red Cross's secretary, Percy Lane Oliver, that he set up the world's first blood transfusion donor service. In the first year Oliver's four volunteers had one call for blood. Within five years the panel's 400 members had over 700 call-outs. Soon Oliver had a network of panels in London that eventually became the National Blood Transfusion Service, a life-saving institution copied worldwide.

HE PASSED THE TEST

Alan Turing was a brilliant English mathematician and computer science pioneer, known as the 'father of artificial intelligence'. He spent World War II cracking German cipher codes and then moved on to computing, developing the idea of the algorithm and computation and paving the way for modern computers. Today in 1950, he published a famous paper on artificial intelligence in which he proposed the Turing test: if a machine can answer questions so well that a questioner cannot tell it is not human, then it can be said to have intelligence. No machine has passed the Turing test. Yet …

MARMALADE SANDWICH, MR GRUBER?

London is the only city in the world to have a mainline station named after a marmalade-loving bear. Oh, come on, let's pretend it's that way round. Polite, but possessing a very hard stare, the duffle coat-clad stowaway from Darkest Peru with a battered hat and suitcase has been a favourite since his first story appeared today in 1958. Author Michael Bond spotted a lone teddy on a shelf in a shop near the station one Christmas Eve. Happily he rescued him. Now, shall we rename Euston as 'Pooh Station'?

MADE IN DAGENHAM

The Ford Dagenham car plant may not be glamorous, but it has gone down in history. The world's most advanced car factory when it opened today in 1931, it had its own power station and steel foundry. It has made over 10,980,368 cars and 37,000,000 engines, and is still the largest diesel engine manufacturing site in the world. It once had the largest neon sign in Europe. And it was thanks to a strike in 1968 by women sewing machinists at the plant that we got the Equal Pay Act of 1970.

IN AN EMERGENCY, TELEGRAPH 999

If you were injured in London in the 1870s, it would likely be a taxi driver who took you to the nearest hospital, on a wheeled stretcher called a 'litter'. The first proper metropolitan ambulance fleet was established today in 1883 at Deptford, although it still wasn't that nippy, being horse-drawn. Today the London Ambulance Service is officially the busiest and largest in the world, with 5,000 staff in 70 stations and 900 ambulances handling 1.6 emergency calls a year (4,380 per day).

THE SOUTH BANK SHOW MUST GO ON

Drama, prostitution and bear-baiting were the principal sources of fun on the South Bank in the Middle Ages. Fast forward a few hundred years and the area is still one of the world's foremost entertainment centres, albeit with skateboarders instead of bears. The Southbank Centre includes the Royal Festival Hall, the Queen Elizabeth Hall and the Hayward Gallery, while the National Theatre and BFI London are nearby. The foundation stone for the Festival Hall was laid today in 1949, and the area has been swarming with theatre-goers, tourists and romantic comedy film crews ever since.

NEW MUSICAL EXPRESS TRAIN

On this misty autumn morning back in 1961, an 18-year-old LSE student called Michael stepped onto platform 2 at Dartford station clutching some of his beloved blues records. A few minutes later, a 17-year-old art student called Keith stepped onto the same platform carrying a Höfner electric guitar. The music-mad young men got chatting. By the time Michael got off his train at Charing Cross, he'd invited Keith to join his band, Little Boy Blue and the Blue Boys. Within a year that would become the Rolling Stones and the world of rock 'n' roll would never be the same again.

167

HOW TO SCREW UP AND STILL SUCCEED

Archimedes invented the screw pump over 2,000 years ago, but without a compact power source, it was no use as a propulsion device. Fast-forward to the 19th century and early steamships used paddles to move. Then Francis Pettit Smith of Hendon, a farmer who taught himself engineering, patented screw propulsion. Smith later built the world's first successful screw-propelled steamship, the SS *Archimedes*, which was launched today in 1838. His screw proved cheaper, lighter, smaller and more efficient than paddles.

IT'S ALL RELATIVE

Albert Einstein authored the *Theory of Relativity*, but the man who explained it to the rest of the world was Sir Arthur Stanley Eddington. Made Astronomer Royal at Greenwich Observatory today in 1913, Eddington became the Brian Cox of his day (except he never played keyboards in a pop band). He used the solar eclipse of 1919 to confirm *Relativity*'s predictions that gravity bends light, and his lucid articles explained Einstein's brain-melting ideas to mere mortals. Which wasn't easy. On being asked if it was true that only three people truly understood *Relativity*, Eddington mused, 'I wonder who the third might be.'

CURRY CAPITAL

The curry house is one of the world's favourite restaurant experiences, and the first outside the Indian subcontinent opened on this day in London in 1810. The Hindoostanee Coffee House was the dream of Indian traveller and entrepreneur Sake Dean Mahomed. Unfortunately, our genteel classes weren't ready for rogan josh, and the venture soon closed. But Mahomed had another Indian ace up his sleeve, and promptly introduced England to 'shampooing' – a form of aromatherapy. This was massively successful and he was even appointed shampooing surgeon to King George III.

BOLLARDS TO THE FRENCH

You might curse bollards when you're trying to get parked, but really they're rather wonderful, as they remind the French of where they stand in life. That's because London's first bollards were French cannons captured at the Battle of Trafalgar, today in 1805. They were put on street corners to stop iron-wheeled carts from mounting the kerbs. When the real cannons were used up, copies were made in a similar shape. But there is still an original French cannon on the South Bank near to Shakespeare's Globe. Très bien.

OCTOBER

JUMP ON, FALL OFF

The red Routemaster bus is one of the most recognisable symbols of London. And the double-decker with the open platform became an icon for a good reason: they were extremely well made. The Routemaster made its first appearance at the Earl's Court Motor Show today in 1954, and many were still winding their picturesque way through the capital's streets almost half a century later. It wasn't until December 2005 that the last full service finished, with the very last bus being a number 159 from Marble Arch to Streatham.

FARTING LANE

In an outstanding example of Victorian resourcefulness, an engineer called Joseph Webb had the brilliant, if rather icky, idea of fuelling London's streetlamps with sewer gas. The first Patent Sewer Ventilating Lamp was installed today in 1895, and hundreds more followed. All were connected to the sewer and burned off the stench of biogas to keep London lit at night. There is still one lamp left, in Carting Lane, which is powered by the high-octane effluent of guests at the nearby Savoy Hotel.

(LAST) FLIGHT OF THE CONCORDES

It was the end of an era at Heathrow today in 2003. No, the queue for the X-ray machines wasn't fully cleared – the legendary supersonic aircraft, Concorde touched down at the end of her last commercial passenger flight. There were tears aplenty, and not just from the rock stars who liked breakfast in Chelsea and lunch in Manhattan. Topping Mach 2 (1,350mph/2,173kph) and crossing the Atlantic in just 3½ hours, Concorde had given us 27 years of super-glamorous supersonic history.

THE RAIN KING

Thanks to our weather there's one thing we absolutely do better than anyone else in the world – make umbrellas. And the trade's master craftsman is James Smith and Sons on New Oxford Street. The world's oldest umbrella shop, it was founded today in 1830; William Gladstone got out of his coach and stepped over the cobbles to get his brolly here. This Victorian emporium is a true time machine, with the finest umbrellas, shooting sticks and canes still made in the basement to the highest of standards. And put up the moment the customer walks out of the door.

FOOTBALL KICKS OFF

On this dark Monday evening in 1863, some gentlemen met in the Freemasons' Tavern near Holborn to standardise the laws of the game that would rule the world – soccer. For the Football Association was established by the football-mad chaps that very night, and the rules agreed soon after. The game was a little hardier then – you could legally hack a player to the ground with a sharp kick to the shins if you wanted to. And rolling around like a big girl's blouse afterwards was very much frowned upon.

YE OLDE GRANDE LATTE

Coffee shops were all the rage in London in 1688 (funny how fashions come round again …) and Edward Lloyd decided to cash in by opening one on Tower Street on this day. Lloyd's Coffee House became a popular haunt of weary seafarers, who Lloyd supplied with the latest shipping news. Shipowners and agents then began coming to Lloyd's to discuss insurance deals. This led to the founding of the world-famous insurance market Lloyd's of London as well as Lloyd's Register.

A BOLD ALTERNATIVE
TO GOVERNMENT BONDS

St Mary Overie Dock on Bankside has been home to the *Golden Hinde*, one of the most famous ships in the world, since this day in 1996. It's a replica of the vessel Sir Francis Drake used to circumnavigate the globe – and pull off the greatest heist in all history. In 1759, when Drake captured the Spanish galleon *Nuestra Señora de la Concepción*, he bagged the largest treasure haul ever: 80lb (36.3kg) of gold, 13 chests of plate and 26 tons of silver. He returned home a national hero: Queen Elizabeth I's share was enough to pay off the entire national debt and have £40,000 left over.

BIRD-BRAINED

When the London Array was switched on today in 2012 it was the largest wind farm of its type in the world. And if you're wondering why you haven't spotted it, that's not because it's in deepest darkest Peckham, but because it's 12 miles (19.3km) offshore in the Thames Estuary. Its 175 turbines do supply London with 630MW of carbon-free electricity, though. This reduces CO_2 emissions by 900,000 tons a year, equal to the gunk from 300,000 cars. The Array would have been even bigger, but a few daft birds flew into it and got themselves chopped up. Idiots.

SCOTT'S GOING ON

Ronnie Scott's Jazz Club first opened its Gerrard Street doors to hep cats today in 1959. It later moved to Frith Street, but the idea was the same: the coolest names in jazz, such as Chet Baker, Ella Fitzgerald and Nina Simone, all introduced by Ronnie's legendary banter. It's known as the world's most famous jazz club, but it was also where Jimi Hendrix gave his last live performance, in 1970. And in 1969, where The Who premiered their rock opera *Tommy*.

OUR HOUSE

Did you know that Jimi Hendrix and George Frideric Handel lived in the same Mayfair house (not at the same time of course)? If you do, it's probably thanks to London's blue plaques scheme, which links famous figures and the buildings they lived and worked in. The first plaque was erected today in 1867 to mark Lord Byron's birthplace at 24 Holles Street, and a further 880 have been put up since. The scheme was the first of its kind and has inspired many other schemes across the world. Interestingly, Handel rented the whole house for £60 a year; Jimi got an attic flat for £30 a week.

NOVEMBER

TOP SECRET CELLARS

One of the most magnificent buildings ever created was Whitehall Palace, which covered 23 acres (9.3ha) and was the largest palace in Europe by 1691. It far outshone Versailles and the Vatican in grandeur, with 1,500 rooms, four tennis courts, bowling greens, a jousting tiltyard and a cock-fighting pit (aptly, on the site of today's Cabinet Office). Whitehall Palace was where Henry VIII lived and died, and where Shakespeare first performed *The Tempest* on this night in 1611. A fire in 1698 left only the Banqueting House above ground, and Henry's VIII's vast wine cellars below. Happily for the MoD, these are now in their basement.

BOX OFFICE RECORD-BREAKER

It's been the home of more glamorous movie premières than you can shake a red carpet at – the Odeon Leicester Square. It opened today in 1937 as the flagship of the Odeon chain and it is still the largest single-screen cinema in the United Kingdom, with 1,679 seats. It's one of the few cinemas with its circle and stalls intact, had the UK's first wide screen and the first digital projector. Last time I was there it was also leading the country in how much it is possible to charge for a box of popcorn.

THE VERY LAST PLACE TO GO SHOPPING

It's Europe's busiest shopping street, and that's despite no sane Londoner ever going there. Yes, welcome to Oxford Street. Which, on a Saturday, is like the Black Hole of Calcutta but with really poor buskers and a Topshop. Its 300 shops stretch for 1½ miles (2.4km) and it's no coincidence that this was the route to the gallows for prisoners being executed at Tyburn, until today in 1783. Most Londoners will avoid it at all costs, but then you find yourself needing a 'Keep Calm and Carry On' mug and a Union Jack meerkat, and where else are you going to go?

BACK TO NATURE

Pulsars, plate tectonics, the ozone hole, nuclear fission, the structure of DNA, cloning and the human genome sequence, all have one thing in common – the world first heard about these scientific breakthroughs in the pages of *Nature*. First published on this day in 1869, in London, it's the world's most-cited scientific publication and getting your research paper into it is a big, big deal. The journal's name came from a line by famous English Romantic poet William Wordsworth: 'To the solid ground of nature trusts the Mind that builds for aye.'

GOING OUT WITH A BANG

It's meant to be a celebration of the survival of our glorious political leaders, but really it's just an excuse to let off some whizz-bangs. Guy Fawkes Night remembers the defeat of the gunpowder plot of 1605, when Fawkes attempted to blow up King James I but was caught red-handed with barrels of gunpowder in a cellar under the House of Lords. Sentenced to death, he escaped the agony of being hung, drawn and quartered by jumping from the scaffold and breaking his own neck.

WE HAVE THE LEFT OF WAY

Driving on the left is right, we all know that. This English 'rule of the road' dates to the times when your greatest danger on the highway was a sword attack, and it paid to be able to have your own sword arm (the right in most people) near your potential foe. The ancient Greeks, Romans, Egyptians and even New York drove on the left until 1804. French trains still run on the left track, because we built most of them. Here, it was enshrined in a law ordering traffic to keep left on the crowded London Bridge, today in 1756. So basically, we're correct – right is wrong.

MAKE YOUR VOTE COUNT (79 TIMES)

The City of London is unique in the world when it comes to democracy, for most of its voters aren't people at all, but businesses. In 1801, the City had 130,000 residents, but now it's only 7,000. However, since the City of London (Ward Elections) Act was passed today in 2002, it has had 32,000 registered voters – because here companies can vote. And the bigger the company, the more votes they get – the largest firms have 79 votes each. This might seem a teensy bit unfair, but it seems to work: the City's Corporation is the world's oldest continuously elected local government body.

PUTTING THE FUN INTO FASHION

8 Mary Quant was a trained milliner who founded her own clothes shop, Bazaar, on the King's Road today in 1955. It was based on the idea of making fun, youthful clothes for young people, which was totally radical for the time. Her fashion liberated a generation: it was Quant who made the miniskirt into a sensation, naming it after her favourite car. She raised eyebrows as well as hemlines, and, for an eye-popping encore, she created hot pants. Quant also invented the modern duvet.

NOT SHORT ON IDEAS

9 Railway arches are where you go to get a dodgy MOT, not world-leading aerospace technology. But that's where the pioneering Short brothers set up shop today in 1908. Horace, Oswald and Eustace started out making balloons before switching to the exciting new technology of aeroplanes under a railway arch by Battersea gas works. Shorts was the first company in the world to make production aircraft, and built the world's first successful twin-engine aircraft. They also designed some of the most successful flying boats in the 1950s. Shorts is still a major aerospace manufacturer, supplying advanced components and control systems. Not from an arches lock-up though.

LIFE DRAWING

William Hogarth (born today in 1697) was an artist who had a gift for caricaturing the drunks, prostitutes, gamblers and hypocrites he saw in the chaotic streets of our 18th century metropolis. He produced paintings and engravings in a series, each episode telling part of an overall story – usually of moral decay – such as 'The Rake's Progress'. His work was a major influence on Fielding and Dickens, and he pretty much pioneered what we think of as the modern cartoon. He's also got a road junction named after him – the Hogarth Roundabout.

POP-UP GOES DOWN

Pop-up restaurants might seem like a new and slightly annoying thing, but they've been going since today in 1827. Fittingly enough, the first was a publicity stunt – engineer Isambard Kingdom Brunel's bold Thames Tunnel had flooded earlier in the year and, to reassure the public about its repairs, he organised the world's first underground dining experience. For this lavish banquet the tunnel was draped in crimson, long candlelit tables were covered in white damask and set with silver and crystal, and the Coldstream Guards' regimental band accompanied the meal for 50 guests (and 120 miners). And not a burger in sight.

THE START OF RECORDED HISTORY

From The Beatles to Pink Floyd, Radiohead to Lady Gaga, the list of bands that have recorded at Abbey Road is a who's who of world music. EMI bought number 3 Abbey Road, St John's Wood, London, in 1929 and spent two years transforming it into the world's first custom-built recording studio. Today in 1931, Sir Edward Elgar conducted his famous recording of 'Land of Hope and Glory', played by the London Symphony Orchestra in Studio One, and Abbey Road was on its way to becoming the most famous recording studio in the world.

ALL ABOARD THE DEATH EXPRESS

You might not be surprised to hear that in the 1850s, London had a housing crisis – but this was for dead people. The growing city's graveyards were full to bursting: one cemetery in Clerkenwell designed for 1,000 bodies had 80,000. So Parliament created a new cemetery at Brookwood, Surrey, which opened to the public (alive and dead) today in 1854. This was the largest in the world, and is still the biggest in Europe, with more than 235,000 people buried there. It even had its own railway, served by the London Necropolis station by Waterloo at one end and two stations in the cemetery itself.

NOVEMBER

THE ORIGINAL WACKY RACES

It was a wet Saturday in 1896 when 54 cars (then brand new) went for a spin (named The Emancipation Run) to celebrate the raising of the speed limit and the scrapping of the escort with a red flag. But it was today's re-enactment in 1927 that made the London–Brighton car run the historic event it still is today. Organisers insisted cars must be pre-1905, thereby establishing the London to Brighton Veteran Car Run, now the longest running, and probably the slowest, motoring event in the world.

DIG FOR VICTORY

You can't build a tunnel under a river – so the world's wisest engineers thought in the early 19th century. 'Balls!' said Marc Isambard Brunel and his son Isambard Kingdom, and using a specially devised tunnelling shield, they completed the Thames Tunnel at Rotherhithe today in 1841. It was the world's very first under-river crossing. To offset the heavy project costs, 800 sightseers a day were allowed to visit the digging face for a shilling. Not something the Crossrail boys are likely to do. The Brunels' tunnel is still in use today, as part, ironically, of the London Overground.

ARMEZ, EN JOUE, FEU!

16 Not many people know that the National Rifle Association was founded on Wimbledon Common. No, not the camo-wearing, spittle-spraying American NRA, its far more civilised British predecessor. Formed to train marksmen to be able to hit Frenchmen, should they invade, the first rifle was cocked today in 1859. Wimbledon got a bit busier over the next few years – bloody tennis players everywhere – which made having a rifle range there a little dangerous. So the Association moved to Bisley in Surrey, where its competitions have been held ever since. Although no Frenchman has yet been bagged.

ENFIELD SETS ITS SIGHTS ON SUCCESS

17 When it comes to making hand-held killing machines, nowhere on Earth can match the achievements of Enfield. For it was here that the Lee-Enfield .303 military bolt-action rifle, the standard British Army rifle from today in 1895 until 1957, was made. Over 17 million were built, many of which are still used in India, Bangladesh and Canada, making this the longest-serving rifle of its type in history. The Royal Small Arms Factory in Enfield was also the home of the Bren and Sten machine guns, which killed people even faster.

SO THAT'S HOW GEORGE OSBORNE GOT THE JOB

Hatton Garden is one of the world's largest jewellery centres with over 300 businesses and 55 jewellery shops. It's the home of De Beers, the firm that has long dominated the world diamond trade. It's been in the gem trade since medieval times and it owes its name to Sir Christopher Hatton (knighted today in 1577). This hugely wealthy noble was quite a mover and shaker. He put up the cash for Francis Drake's famous round-the-world voyage, and Elizabeth I was so impressed by his dancing that she made him Chancellor.

IDEAL LIVING

Dreaming your tatty old flat is a stylish, spacious abode is a national pastime – but it's nothing new. Our obsession with home makeover shows like *Grand Designs* and *DIY SOS* can be traced back to this day in 1908, when the inaugural Ideal Home Exhibition opened at Olympia's Grand Hall in Kensington. The event was initially cooked up as a marketing stunt for the *Daily Mail*, which sponsored it for 100 years. It is now the biggest home show in the world.

IS THAT A TICKET IN-SPECTRE?

The Tube is full of ghostly apparitions going nowhere – and that's just the stations. London's Underground is the global capital of ghost stations, with more than 40. They died for various reasons: Bull & Bush on the Northern Line was never even used following its completion in 1906. Down Street in Mayfair closed in 1932 because toffs didn't use it. Aldwych was on a branch line from Holborn – a station that it was quicker to walk to. Charing Cross's Jubilee Line station closed today in 1999 when the line was expanded. Like many stations, this lives on as a filming location: *Skyfall*'s Tube crash was shot here, as the rushing crowds passed unaware just feet away.

ECCENTRI-CITY

England is famously a nation of eccentrics, so it's only right that our capital city should have the world's finest collection of weirdos. Of course, this being England, our eccentrics are sociable and organised – they even formed their own society, the Eccentric Club, today in 1890. The clock in their bar runs backwards (an idea we can all get behind), insist on non-conformist thinking and have the Duke of Edinburgh as their patron. Which actually makes total sense.

NOVEMBER

THE BEST BREAD SINCE SLICED BREAD

British wheat used to be so low in protein it didn't actually make good bread. Then bakers in a research lab in Chorleywood found that by chucking extra yeast and hard fats (and some chemicals) into the dough and pulverising it in massive high-speed mixers, you could make bread that was 40 per cent softer, cheaper, and lasted twice as long. And make it in just 3½ hours. Chorleywood bread was first sliced today in 1961, and now 80 per cent of Britain's bread is baked this way. It's also the standard method in Australia, New Zealand, India and many other countries. Pass the butter.

HERE'S LOOKING AT YOU ...

Artist Anna Maria Grosholtz's first subject was Voltaire, and she completed his likeness today in 1777. But she really mastered her art during the French Revolution when she fetched the decapitated heads of executed citizens out of the basket and made their death masks. Charming lady. She later married a Monsieur Tussaud and moved to London, where she established a waxwork museum on Baker Street. She then added murderers, criminals and general celebrities to the gallery of decapitees. Winston Churchill has had the most likenesses made – 11.

THE MASTER OF INTERIOR DESIGN

'Have nothing in your houses that you do not know to be useful, or believe to be beautiful.' So thought William Morris from Walthamstow, an artist who transformed just about every creative field he worked in. His novel *The Wood Beyond the World* (published today in 1894) was the first to be set in an entirely invented fantasy world, inspiring C.S. Lewis and J.R.R. Tolkien. He was a major force in the founding of socialism in Britain, and in his spare time he translated Classic and Icelandic literature. His wallpaper, fabrics and furniture were hand-made, of supreme quality, and just about as far from IKEA as it's possible to get.

THEY FED THE WORLD

On this day in 1984, Bob Geldof and 43 other members of Band Aid gathered in a London recording studio to sing 'Do They Know it's Christmas'. They hoped it might raise £70,000 for famine-stricken Ethiopia; it became the biggest-selling single in UK chart history, shifting 3.5 million copies and raising millions of pounds. That was just the start of the positive impact that Band Aid had around the world. In 2005, the massive Live 8 concert in Hyde Park aimed to highlight the continuing struggle in Africa 20 years after the original Live Aid concert.

DON'T GROUSE ABOUT THE PRICE

J. Purdey and Sons are to shotguns as Savile Row tailors are to suits – the best in the world. In the bang business in Mayfair since today in 1814, Purdey have produced bespoke guns perfectly suited to your stature and shooting style. This craftsmanship does take time (two years), and a little bit of money – a Purdey gun starts at around £70,000. Although your Lordship will of course need to buy a pair – when the birds fly thick, a 'loader' stands behind you ready to take your empty gun and hand you a loaded one.

NO, WE DON'T DO CORNROWS

Trust a London barber to make shaving into an art form. Geo. F. Trumper ('Trumpers' to those in the know) in Mayfair has been pruning the most respected beards in Britain since today in 1875. In this mahogany-panelled palace of preening you can get a haircut, buy grooming aids and have a hairpiece discreetly fitted in a curtained booth at the back. So skilled are the barbers here that Johnny Depp came to brush up his technique before shooting *Sweeney Todd: The Demon Barber of Fleet Street* – the shaving part of the job, that is, not the baking-customers-into-pies bit.

IN ENGLAND'S GREEN AND PLEASANT LAND

Born today in 1757 in Broadwick Street, William Blake was a professional engraver who became one of the world's truly visionary artists. And he really did see visions – hallucinations of angels, his dead brother, God and the ghosts of fleas. Blake stayed just the right side of mad, however, and works like *The Tyger*, *The Lamb* and *The Ancient of Days* would profoundly influence artists as varied as Aldous Huxley, Bob Dylan and Philip Pullman. Blake also wrote the words to that classic of Englishness, 'Jerusalem'.

ARCHERS START SHOOTING

In Dorset House, Gloucester Place, The Archers spent their most productive years. Not the radio serial, but the film production company started by Michael Powell and Emeric Pressburger. As writers, producers and directors Powell and Pressburger took total creative control to make films that were far ahead of their time. They released 24 films between this day in 1939 and 1972, including hits such as *The Red Shoes*, *Black Narcissus* and *A Matter of Life and Death* (premiered today in 1946). These had a major influence on later film-makers including Martin Scorsese and Francis Ford Coppola, while David Lean learned his trade as an editor there.

FICTIONAL FORENSICS

More crimes have been brilliantly solved by London detectives than those of any other city. Of course, we're not talking about Scotland Yard here, but the fictional roster of crime busters that includes Hercule Poirot, Lord Peter Wimsey and, of course, Sherlock Holmes. He first appeared in *A Study in Scarlet* in the 1887 issue of *Beeton's Christmas Annual* (published today). The residence of this most brilliant of all detectives, at 221B Baker Street, attracts thousands of tourists a year, many of whom do not seem to realise that Holmes was not a real person.

DECEMBER

TRADITIONAL CHRISTMAS
MONEY-MAKER

You can thank London artist John Callcott Horsley for that stack of cards with robins on spade handles cluttering up your mantelpiece. For it was he who created the first ever Christmas card, in 1843. Even then it was a commercial enterprise – he was commissioned by Sir Henry Cole, who had helped introduce the Penny Post three years earlier. Two batches of 2,050 cards went on sale today at a shilling each. Although popular, Horsley's design was controversial because it featured a toddler gulping wine. A bit too much Christmas spirit, there.

PICTURE PERFECT

2 Established today in 1856, the National Portrait Gallery is the oldest portrait gallery in the world. It was created thanks to 10 years of campaigning by Philip Henry Stanhope, 5th Earl Stanhope. The first picture in the collection was the famous 'Chandos' portrait of Shakespeare. It also has the world's largest collection of portraits – over 195,000 of the greatest names in British history, in fact. The Gallery has always been a historical institution: whether a portrait should be included in the collection or not is judged on the status of the sitter, not the quality of the art. So why they have a picture of Posh Spice is anyone's guess.

THE LADIES' BRIDGE

Waterloo Bridge is the only major bridge in the world built mostly by women. In World War II so many men were away fighting that tens of thousands of women were drafted into construction projects to keep the country's roads, canals, trains and bridges running. After surviving German bomb damage, the elegant new Thames crossing was opened today in 1945. By the end of the war 25,000 women were employed as brickies, labourers and joiners. But were they leaning from the scaffolding and whistling at the boys, we ask ourselves?

HERITAGE HEAVEN

World Heritage Sites are the planet's most physically or culturally remarkable places as recognised by UNESCO. Impressively, London is home to four world heritage sites, which is more than most whole countries have. UNESCO has recognised the cultural sites of Maritime Greenwich (inscribed today in 1997), the Royal Botanical Gardens at Kew, the Palace of Westminster and Westminster Abbey including St Margaret's Church, and the Tower of London (murdering princes being an important part of our culture).

SOLD TO THE MAN WITH THE NERVOUS TWITCH

James Christie, founder of the famous auction house, brought the hammer down on his first sale today in 1766. He later capitalised on London's new status as the major centre of the international art trade following the French Revolution, building a reputation as the premier auctioneer of fine arts. Christie's has been based at King Street in St James's since 1823.

DECEMBER

STOP, LOOK AND LISTEN
(FOR NEIGHING)

The world's first pedestrian crossing signal was erected in Bridge Street, Westminster. A railway engineer called John Peak Knight realised that with pedestrians, horses and coaches all vying for the same narrow London streets, some sort of control system was required. So he built a signal with a semaphore arm that was raised and lowered by a police constable by rotating a handle. At night, green and red gas lights lit up on the end of the arms. It first turned to red on this day in 1868. And some idiot on a penny-farthing rode through it without stopping approximately 45 seconds later.

THE GOOD SAMARITANS

St Stephen Walbrook in the City is a beautiful Wren church, where an equally beautiful idea was born. Its vicar Chad Varah was so moved by the suicide of a 14-year-old girl that he launched The Samaritans here, today in 1953. The Samaritans was the country's first ever 24-hour telephone helpline, and it grew from a few helpers in St Stephen's crypt to 20,600 trained volunteers in 203 branches, taking five million calls for help a year.

THE RAC REVS INTO ACTION

8 Inaugurated today in 1897, the Royal Automobile Club has done much to shape the motoring history of our country. In 1905, the Club organised the first Tourist Trophy (TT) motorcycle race, making that the world's oldest regularly run motor race. It also organised the first British Grand Prix in 1926. The Club introduced driving certificates in 1905, 30 years before the government decided to get involved. It also has one of the largest and most splendid clubhouses in London, on Pall Mall.

LONDON CLEANS UP ITS ACT

9 Sometimes even London's pollution is worth being proud of. In December 1952 a pool of cold air was trapped under a lid of warm air over London, and the smoke from heavy coal-burning produced a fog of blackout density. Visibility fell to a few feet. Public transport stopped. Fog seeped indoors – films were cancelled because audiences couldn't see the screen. There was a lot of stiff upper lip about this 'pea souper' at the time, but about 12,000 people died. Today, after five days of smog, it finally lifted. The good news is it was *so* bad it led to the Clean Air Act, which did what its name suggested and also marked the start of legal moves to protect our environment.

TAKE PRIDE IN LONDON
- DRINK LONDON PRIDE

10 Fuller's has been oiling the throats of thirsty Londoners since this day in 1845. But beer has been brewed on the Chiswick site since at least the 1650s – when London's water was so dirty that even babes drank beer for breakfast. It's the oldest and largest brewery in London – and one of the best in the country. In fact, three Fuller brews (London Pride, ESB and Chiswick Bitter) have been named Champion Beer of Britain. No other brewery has matched that feat. Slightly randomly, the brewery also boasts the UK's oldest wisteria plant, brought here from China in 1816.

BEST FOR BIG BUSINESS

11 We all know London is a major business centre, but its financial performance really is something to be proud of. London has 12.5 per cent of the UK's population, but generates 22 per cent of its GDP (according to a report published today in 2013). Over 100 of Europe's 500 largest companies are headquartered in London and the city's economy is bigger than those of Sweden and Belgium. Every day, more US dollars are traded in London than in New York, and more Euros traded than in every other city in Europe combined. No wonder everything is so expensive.

IT'S A LET IF IT GOES IN THE SHERRY

Shoreditch drinkers won't be surprised to know that table tennis owes its existence to London hipsters – albeit of the Victorian variety. When cool young things amused themselves after dinner by using paddles made of cigar box lids to bash balls carved from champagne corks across their dining tables, the game soon took off. 'Ping Pong' was the name of a brand of equipment for playing the game. The Table Tennis Association was formed in London today in 1901, and the first official World Championships were held here in 1926. Although not on someone's dining table.

DECEMBER

WHICH BLOB IS NEWMAN AND WHICH IS BADDIEL?

There was a time, before tonight in 1993, when the biggest joke at a live comedy show wasn't the ticket price. Then Robert Newman and David Baddiel got so popular that they sold out the 12,000-seat Wembley Arena and played the world's first stand-up stadium gig. And now we seem to be happy to pay £45 to watch a mildly amusing speck in the distance while sipping a £7 pint. So take pride, Londoners, it's thanks to us that tens of thousands of people can now be simultaneously delighted by Michael McIntyre.

USE YOUR DOME

The Millennium Dome, New Labour's £850m vanity project, was once the butt of endless jokes. But today in 2008 it had the last laugh when it earned a place in history as the world's most popular entertainment venue. Over two million people rock out here every year, more than at Madison Square Garden. The O_2 arena stands inside the Dome and is the largest structure of its kind in the world – you could easily lose the Great Pyramid at Giza inside. Although it would play merry hell with the acoustics.

HOOKER'S HERBAL HOTHOUSE

William Hooker was a revolutionary botanist who developed the royal pleasure grounds at Kew into the world's foremost botanic gardens. Starting today in 1841, he expanded the gardens from 30 to 70 acres (12.1 to 28.3ha) and the arboretum to 300 acres (121ha), had many new glasshouses erected and established a museum of economic botany. Kew has the world's largest collection of living plants (over 30,000); research here has helped the commercial cultivation of bananas, coffee and tea, and has led to the production of many useful drugs, including quinine to help combat malaria.

TECHNICALLY,
THAT'S A BIG FAT GREY ONE

We have enough of the blooming things, so it makes sense that a Londoner should name them. Today in 1802, Luke Howard classified the different types of clouds. His basic terms were: *cumulus* (meaning heap), *stratus* (meaning layer), and *cirrus* (meaning curl), with various sub-categories. His bright idea of using Latin meant his terms transcended national boundaries, and meteorologists still use his system 200 years later.

Howard also suggested that clouds form for a reason, and so founded the science of weather prediction. Which we're not so brilliant at.

ONE MAN IS AN ISLAND

He was born plain old Daniel Foe, today in 1660 in St Giles Cripplegate, the son of a tallow chandler. But he went on to become one of the most influential English men of letters ever. The first thing he had the sense to do was add 'De' on to his surname to sound more aristocratic. He then became a successful trader, journalist and pamphleteer, and even a spy against the Scots. He wrote more than 500 books and pamphlets, including the first ever novel (and one of the most famous) in English, *Robinson Crusoe*.

COMPACT AND BIJOU

You might think that laughably small flats are a modern trend in London, but the city has been excelling at this sort of thing for centuries. One of the world's smallest townhouses is number 10 Hyde Park Place, Marble Arch. This is just 3ft 6in (1m) wide – not big enough to feed a cat, let along swing it. Now part of Tyburn Convent, this building was first occupied today in 1805 as a watch house overlooking the nearby St George's graveyard – so a guard could keep an eye on bodysnatchers. Which he did standing up, presumably.

THIS RADIO STATION WILL BE RUBBISH

A radio revolution began today in 1932 with the first transmission of the Empire Service. The first Director General didn't have high hopes for the station, saying 'The programmes will neither be very interesting nor very good.' However, by the end of 1942 broadcasts were being made in all European languages and the renamed 'World Service' was one of the most popular stations in existence. Today it is the world's largest international broadcaster, with 188 million listeners and programmes in 28 languages. There's no advertising and it's even free of annoying DJ posses laughing at each other's jokes.

FROSTY FIRST

20 You might think it's nippy in winter, but in the 17th, 18th and 19th centuries it often got so cold that the Thames froze over. People went skating, set up markets, had horse and coach races, roasted oxen and even led an elephant over the ice in events known as Frost Fairs. A two-month freeze started today in 1683, and a man named Croom set up a printing press to produce souvenir postcards for sixpence featuring the customer's name, the date, and the fact that the card was printed on the Thames. They were wildly popular, with King Charles II even buying one. Croom thereby pioneered the modern postcard, celebrity endorsement and the marketing of tourist tat in one fell swoop.

PARK LIFE

21 What's the largest park in London? Hyde? Regent's? Richmond? Nope, it's Lee Valley Park, which stretches for 26 miles (41.8km) and covers 10,000 acres (4,047ha), making it one of the largest urban parks in the world. Established by a special Act of Parliament today in 1966, it was extended following the 2012 Olympics. The creation of London's newest 'green lung' is remarkable considering much of the area was an industrial wasteland a few decades ago.

DECEMBER

THE PRINCE OF POO

In the 1850s the River Thames was the world's largest open sewer and the streets stank of effluent. The Metropolitan Board of Works (founded today in 1855) asked engineer Joseph Bazalgette to sort it out. He decided to tear up every street in the city and lay a whole new system of waste piping. Realising this could only be done once, he massively over-engineered the project. Over 100 miles (160km) of huge trunk sewers were installed under new river embankments, as well as 1,000 miles (1,600km) of local pipes. And it did the trick: the river came back to life, diseases dwindled and London had a model sewage system that still works today.

SATNAV IS FOR SISSIES

London cabbies sometimes get a bit of a rough ride, but 'The Knowledge', the rigorous test of geographical lore that they must pass, is the world's most demanding training course for taxicab drivers. Introduced today in 1865, it requires applicants to memorise 25,000 roads and 320 'runs' across town, as well as all major places of interest. It usually takes two to four years of zooming round on a moped with an A–Z and 12 attempts at the exam to pass. Where to, Guv?

A TREEMENDOUS TRADITION

Christmas Eve is such a magical day in London's year that you can't help but be proud of this great city. Workers leave early to gulp mulled wine and fall on their arse on the ice rinks, people tear about Oxford Street trying to do a week's worth of Christmas shopping in two hours, and commuters bash into carol singers by the Trafalgar Square tree. Christmas trees were unknown in Britain until today in 1832, when the 13-year-old future Queen Victoria had one placed in her room by her German relatives. Delighted, she wrote about it in her journal and encouraged the wider adoption of this festive continental tradition in later life.

GLORY TO GOD IN THE HIGHEST

It's fitting that today we take pride in one of the most majestic churches in the world – St Paul's Cathedral. The present church is the masterpiece of Sir Christopher Wren and it was finally fully open for worship today in 1711, replacing the medieval structure destroyed in the Great Fire of London. It has the world's largest crypt and Britain's biggest bell, Great Paul, which weighs 16½ tons. The magnificent cathedral dome is the third largest in the world, standing 365ft (111m) above the City streets, and is the only one in England.

LONDON STEPS INTO THE LIMELIGHT

The curtain went up in the Covent Garden Theatre tonight in 1837 and the audience gasped – the actors were bathed in dazzling white light. This was the world stage debut of limelight, created by heating a cylinder of lime (calcium oxide, not the citrus fruit) in a flame of oxygen and hydrogen. It was 37 times brighter than the strongest oil lamp and could cast the shadow of a hand on a wall 10 miles (16km) away. As the first practical spotlight it revolutionised stage lighting and Victorian theatre, and was soon beloved of luvvies worldwide.

THE INVENTION THAT REALLY CLEANED UP

What should one wipe with? The Romans in London used sponges on sticks. Lord Chesterfield kept a volume of *Horace* in his pocket at all times and, on sitting down, he would read a couple of pages then tear them out and use them. Rags and newspaper have done the job for the working classes. But the British Perforated Paper Company of Banner Street, London, was the first to really, ahem, take the matter in hand, when it launched its latest product today in 1880. Paper squares boxed fresh and ready – the first modern loo roll.

CAN'T BLOODY MOVE FOR ALL THESE KINGS AND QUEENS

The wonderful Westminster Abbey, the largest and most important Gothic church in Britain, was consecrated today in 1065. Although, technically, it's not an abbey at all, but a Royal Peculiar, a church under direct jurisdiction of the monarch. The next year saw the coronation of both King Harold and his usurper William the Conqueror, and since then all 40 English and British monarchs have been crowned on the hallowed but rather uncomfy-looking St Edward's Chair. Most are also buried here, and there have been 16 royal weddings: from Henry and Matilda in 1100 to Will and Kate in 2011.

DEAD RINGERS

If your beloved Fluffy passes away and you can't bear to be without him, you can always pop up to Islington and have him turned into a doorstop. Get Stuffed is not just one of the world's finest taxidermists, it's an English institution that's gone right through 'rather eccentric' and out the other side into 'hilariously disturbing'. Opened today in 1974, this emporium of the expired will happily preserve any pooch, puss, parrot – or indeed an emu, should you happen to keep one of those. Totally barking.

UP THE JUNCTION

For most travellers, Clapham Junction is where you start putting your *Metro* away, but actually it's a station to be proud of. Every day 2,000 trains trundle through here, up to 180 an hour, with 430,000 commuters aboard, making it the busiest station in Europe by train numbers. It is also the UK's largest station, counting all its sidings. The only thing wrong with this modern transport wonder is its name: Clapham Junction is not in Clapham, but in Battersea. This is because when the line through here was completed today in 1860, Battersea was a bit of a dump.

JUST THE TONIC

The East India Company was chartered in London today in 1600 by Queen Elizabeth I. This organisation has something of a chequered history (at one point it imported more than 1,400 tons of opium a year into China), but, on the flipside, it did give the world the quintessentially English tipple – the gin and tonic. Realising quinine helped prevent malaria, the company's officers consumed large quantities of tonic water, which is loaded with this beneficial drug. To improve the taste, it was of course, necessary to also add medicinal quantities of gin. And ice, and lemon. Oh, and a sprig of mint…